Trouble in the Big House . . .

"Shut your trap, Meskin. I ain't talkin' to you."

"I'm not looking for a fight," Slocum said. He rubbed his left hand over the spot where his cross-draw holster usually hung. He felt naked without his Colt Navy.

"Fight! Fight!" The chant went up, and Slocum knew he couldn't walk away.

"Look, it's this way . . ." He stepped a little closer, then launched a kick aimed at the big man's crotch. Slocum's aim was an inch off, and he caught a heavily muscled inner thigh. The impact hurt his knee and sent him stumbling back. And then he was engulfed in two hundred fifty pounds of smelly, fighting convict.

DON'T MISS THESE
ALL-ACTION WESTERN SERIES
FROM THE BERKLEY PUBLISHING GROUP

***THE GUNSMITH** by J. R. Roberts*
    Clint Adams was a legend among lawmen, outlaws, and la-
    dies. They called him . . . the Gunsmith.

***LONGARM** by Tabor Evans*
    The popular long-running series about Deputy U.S. Marshal
    Custis Long—his life, his loves, his fight for justice.

***SLOCUM** by Jake Logan*
    Today's longest-running action Western. John Slocum rides
    a deadly trail of hot blood and cold steel.

***BUSHWHACKERS** by B. J. Lanagan*
    An action-packed series by the creators of Longarm! The
    rousing adventures of the most brutal gang of cutthroats
    ever assembled—Quantrill's Raiders.

***DIAMONDBACK** by Guy Brewer*
    Dex Yancey is Diamondback, a Southern gentleman turned
    con man when his brother cheats him out of the family for-
    tune. Ladies love him. Gamblers hate him. But nobody pulls
    one over on Dex . . .

***WILDGUN** by Jack Hanson*
    The blazing adventures of mountain man Will Barlow—
    from the creators of Longarm!

***TEXAS TRACKER** by Tom Calhoun*
    J.T. Law: the most relentless—and dangerous—manhunter
    in all Texas. Where sheriffs and posses fail, he's the best
    man to bring in the most vicious outlaws—for a price.

JAKE LOGAN

SLOCUM'S BREAKOUT

JOVE BOOKS, NEW YORK

THE BERKLEY PUBLISHING GROUP
Published by the Penguin Group
Penguin Group (USA) Inc.
375 Hudson Street, New York, New York 10014, USA
Penguin Group (Canada), 90 Eglinton Avenue East, Suite 700, Toronto, Ontario M4P 2Y3, Canada
(a division of Pearson Penguin Canada Inc.)
Penguin Books Ltd., 80 Strand, London WC2R 0RL, England
Penguin Group Ireland, 25 St. Stephen's Green, Dublin 2, Ireland (a division of Penguin Books Ltd.)
Penguin Group (Australia), 250 Camberwell Road, Camberwell, Victoria 3124, Australia
(a division of Pearson Australia Group Pty. Ltd.)
Penguin Books India Pvt. Ltd., 11 Community Centre, Panchsheel Park, New Delhi—110 017, India
Penguin Group (NZ), 67 Apollo Drive, Rosedale, Auckland 0632, New Zealand
(a division of Pearson New Zealand Ltd.)
Penguin Books (South Africa) (Pty.) Ltd., 24 Sturdee Avenue, Rosebank, Johannesburg 2196,
South Africa

Penguin Books Ltd., Registered Offices: 80 Strand, London WC2R 0RL, England

This is a work of fiction. Names, characters, places, and incidents either are the product of the author's imagination or are used fictitiously, and any resemblance to actual persons, living or dead, business establishments, events, or locales is entirely coincidental

SLOCUM'S BREAKOUT

A Jove Book / published by arrangement with the author

PRINTING HISTORY
Jove edition / November 2011

Copyright © 2011 by Penguin Group (USA) Inc.
Cover illustration by Sergio Giovine.

ISBN: 978-0-515-15011-7

JOVE®
Jove Books are published by The Berkley Publishing Group,
a division of Penguin Group (USA) Inc.,
375 Hudson Street, New York, New York 10014.
JOVE® is a registered trademark of Penguin Group (USA) Inc.
The "J" design is a trademark of Penguin Group (USA) Inc.

PRINTED IN THE UNITED STATES OF AMERICA

10 9 8 7 6 5 4 3 2 1

1

"No talkin'!" A rifle butt struck John Slocum in the shoulder and knocked him to his knees. He clanked the chains on his wrists and balled his fists as he looked up at the blue-uniformed guard. The man towered over him. Seeing the hatred in Slocum's green eyes, the guard stepped away and leveled his rifle. His finger tightened on the trigger. For two cents he would put a slug into Slocum's head and not think twice about it.

"I'm getting up," Slocum said. He put his hands down in the dry California dirt and levered himself erect. It was harder than he'd anticipated because the chains connecting the shackles on his ankles allowed only eighteen inches of play. Walking was impossible; he had to shuffle.

"Hurry it up. You're keepin' the wagon waitin'."

"Wouldn't want that, now would we?" came a voice just loud enough for the guard to hear. The prison guard swung around, his rifle hunting for a target.

"Who said that? Who's talkin' when I tole you all to shut yer pie holes?"

Slocum shuffled forward with the other ten men, all

1

shackled and looking as if they could chew through their chains and kill, given the chance. Slocum snorted. Most of them had killed somebody. That was how they had ended up in the line of prisoners being herded into the bed of a wagon.

The guard helped Slocum along with another hard blow to the shoulder. Slocum winced but kept walking, head down. This seemed to appease the guard because he hurried on to another prisoner who refused to show any humility at his condition. From the beating the man received, he might not make it to the prison alive.

One prisoner already in the wagon reached out his manacled hands and helped Slocum up.

"Thanks," Slocum said, then shot a quick look back to be sure the guard hadn't heard.

"He's too busy havin' his fun with poor Gordon. But you got the right instinct. Do what those bastards tell you, and you'll get along all right."

"You been in before?" Slocum studied the man seated across from him in the wagon. The pallor gave him away as someone who ventured out but little when the sun was high. That might mean he was a gambler, but his stubby fingers didn't have the dexterity Slocum associated with cardsharps.

"Wasn't out but two weeks 'fore they got me on trumped-up charges. The sheriff don't like me none, the dirt-eatin', mother—" He clamped his mouth shut when the guard hoisted Gordon and threw him facedown into the wagon.

Satisfied he had all the prisoners loaded, he bellowed for the driver to make good time. Slocum watched the guard recede and finally disappear in a cloud of dust as the wagon rattled along the rocky road. The drought had hung on for the entire year. The usual rain in January hadn't come down south, and Slocum had drifted up to San Francisco. As the wagon bumped along, he looked up and saw the foreboding gray stone walls of San Quentin getting closer by the minute.

"Ain't named for a saint," the man opposite him said. "Named after some Injun what was captured on the spot." He shook his head. Slocum saw the sunlight shine off a couple lice migrating through his greasy hair, working their way down to his beard. The man didn't take much notice. "'Magine that, an Injun named Quentin. Belonged to the Miwok tribe. Was a fighter fer Chief Marin back in the day."

"How'd you come to know so much about the history?" Slocum asked. He was growing increasingly apprehensive as he studied the thick stone walls and the alert blue-uniformed guards in the towers at the corners. He was sorry he had agreed to such a crazy scheme as—

"They call me Doc," the other prisoner piped up, interrupting Slocum's growing worry that he had dealt himself into a game that couldn't be won. "I was a professor at a college 'fore I got myself in bad."

Slocum doubted it but said nothing about the man's background. Instead, he asked, "Anybody ever broken out?"

"Oh, sure, there've been a few. Mighty few, I'd say, but it can be done. Them guards is human mostly. They look the other way, and a few clever folks can sneak on out. Need a lot of money to bribe 'em, though, if that's what you got in mind." Doc leaned closer and said in a husky whisper, "You got money?"

"If you've got a way out," Slocum said. "I don't intend staying behind the walls too long."

"Smart man. The longer they got you, the harder it is to get away. They starve you, and some of the unlucky bastards get put in the dungeon. Yup, that's right," Doc said, seeing Slocum's startled expression. "They got theyselves a dungeon, jist like the tyrants over in Europe got in their castles."

"Torture?"

"Not so much, 'less you earn it." Doc looked smug. "Truth is, most new prisoners earn it. Keeps 'em from thinkin' 'bout escapin' later. That's what's known as gentle persuasion."

"What's gentle about it?" Slocum asked.

"They reckon they don't have to hang you, that's gentle."

The heavy gates opened and the wagon rolled through. The brief flash of shadow from the wall caused Slocum to shiver in dread. He liked this less and less, but he realized he had gotten what he deserved for not thinking things through. He should never have listened to Conchita or fallen under her spell. If he had kept riding north, up to Oregon maybe, he wouldn't have spent those nights in the sultry woman's bed and—

He jumped as the gates slammed shut behind him. Slocum watched the guards draw the locking bar into place, then padlock it securely. That lock was as big as his head and would take a stick of dynamite—more!—to open without the key. The wagon pulled around to the side of a three-story building made entirely of stone.

"You kin see San Francisco Bay from the roof," Doc said. "Fact is the south side of the prison fetches up along the shoreline, but don't think to get out that way. Water's colder 'n a witch's tit all year round, and they got guards in boats patrolling outside all the time. A signal goes up and they shoot anything that moves." He chuckled. "They shot 'emselves a shark last time the alarm was sounded."

"A bell?" Slocum asked.

Doc looked at him funny, then nodded. Before he could answer, rough hands grabbed his coat and dragged him out to crash onto the ground. Slocum was similarly treated. The others in the wagon had difficulty keeping their footing, but Doc and Slocum took the brunt of the punishment compared to other prisoners getting down from the wagon.

More than one boot caught Slocum in the back, making movement painful. He cried out when a guard kicked him hard in the side.

"Git up. You ain't gonna lay about all day."

Slocum had learned how to climb to his feet with the shackles and did so. He started to help Doc to his feet, but the guard shoved him away so he could use a truncheon on the prone man. Doc covered up the best he could and waited for the rain of blows to cease. Only then did he get to his feet. Slocum figured that Doc had been through such treatment before and knew how to survive it.

As he and the others shuffled into the building, Slocum damned Conchita Valenzuela and her brother and the hare-brained scheme that had brought him to this point.

Standing in a single file, shuffling forward when the prisoner in front had been processed, Slocum finally reached the desk, where a guard sporting bright gold sergeant's stripes on his uniform sat with a ledger open in front of him. He glanced up at Slocum, then at the book, and ran his finger across a line.

"Jasper Jarvis, in for robbery. Two years."

Slocum said nothing. The sergeant looked up, one bushy eyebrow rising.

"So? That you or not?"

"It's me," Slocum said.

"Get those chains off and into those," the sergeant said as another guard shoved a prison uniform into his hands.

Slocum started to ask how he was supposed to get the chains off when the guard grabbed him and sent him staggering toward an arched doorway. He bounced off one side and then the other, keeping his balance, then saw the prisoner who had been ahead of him at the far end of the stone corridor at an open doorway. The man's hands were already free, and a guard worked to free him from his leg irons. This lent speed to Slocum's shuffle. He wanted out of the shackles as quickly as he could.

Once freed, he went into the room and saw a half-dozen guards, all with rifles trained on the prisoner now shorn of his irons.

"Git yer worthless clothes off and take a shower. Then put your uniform on," the guard said to the prisoner. Clutching his coarse black-striped white canvas prison uniform, Slocum stripped naked, followed the other prisoner into what was closer to a sheep dip than a shower. He came out coughing and eyes watering. With the guards prodding him, he managed to get into the heavy prison garb.

He put up his hand to shield his eyes from the sun, now directly overhead. He was in a yard with dozens of other prisoners.

"You new prisoners will be assigned your cells at the end of exercise. Try not to get killed 'fore then." The guard speaking laughed harshly, making his real intentions known. If every one of the inmates died, he would be just fine with that.

Slocum stumbled around, getting his balance back after being chained for so long. He had been arrested down in San Francisco after Conchita turned him in as Jarvis. They had pored over wanted posters and found one for the wanted convict who had escaped before being sent to San Quentin, ensuring immediate transport to the prison. Best of all, there hadn't been a sketch of Jasper Jarvis.

Slocum had agreed to assume the identity of Jarvis since his crime was relatively minor—he knew that by the twenty-dollar reward. No one was in a hurry to recapture Jarvis, and the ease with which he had been sent to San Quentin proved that. He was a minor annoyance, not a big clap of thunder to rile up everyone.

As he walked around, he got his bearings and studied the walls, the guards, and the security. He saw that Doc hadn't been joking about how difficult it would be to escape unless a lot of money greased a guard's palm. The ground was rocky and would be difficult to tunnel through. The walls were both sturdy and tall. While they might be scaled, it had to be at night. The guards in the towers at each corner of the penitentiary alertly watched their wards below in the yard. That might slack off with time; Slocum had no idea how long the guards had been on duty or if they might catch a few winks when the officers weren't looking.

Chancing on a sleeping guard just as he intended to climb over the wall didn't strike him as a good escape plan.

The sound of the wagon that had brought the prisoners rattling and clanking back out drew his attention.

"Ain't gonna hide in that," came a gruff voice. Slocum looked over, then up. He stood six feet tall. This giant with a bushy beard, tiny, deep-set eyes, and hair so wild it might have been a tuft of black prairie grass loomed above him.

"Didn't want to be so obvious," Slocum said.

"You just got in. All you fish are like that, thinkin' you kin get outta here. You cain't. Live with it. Let 'em release you . . . unless you're in for life."

Slocum's jaw tightened at the idea that an escape attempt might just mean his life. Damn Conchita! Damn his own charity. She had assured him her brother had been locked up on bogus testimony. And then she had added—

"You'll only git tossed into solitary, tryin' to escape. Them guards got their eyes on you, the way you're watchin' the wagon and all."

"Thanks," Slocum said.

"You got a name?"

Slocum almost answered with his own, then caught himself in time and said, "Jarvis."

"Hmph," the giant said. "You got a brother named Jarvis?"

Slocum stepped back a half pace and looked at the mountain of a man.

"Nope," he said. "Why do you ask?"

"I got a bone to pick with Jasper Jarvis, that's why. The sneaky li'l toad got me locked up in here for somethin' he done down in San Francisco." The convict squinted hard at Slocum. "You don't look nuthin' like 'im, so I reckon you ain't kin."

The heavy canvas prison garb turned into a furnace as Slocum sweat. He was having nothing but bad luck.

"You know another prisoner name of José Valenzuela?"

"You got a score to settle with him?"

"Got a message from outside," Slocum said. "Never met him."

"That's him over yonder," the man said. "You watch yer step. He's a Meskin. Cain't trust 'em. Worse 'n Jarvis." With that, the man turned and walked away. Slocum fancied he felt the ground rumble with every step the huge prisoner took. Only when he thought it was safe, Slocum turned and looked in Valenzuela's direction.

A half-dozen Mexicans huddled together but one stood apart. From the description Conchita had given him, that had to be her brother. As he got closer, he saw the pink half-circle scar on his cheek and knew this was José Valenzuela.

A bell rang, and the convicts started moving toward the large central building where they were housed.

"Wait up," Slocum said. "I've got a message for you. From your sister."

"From . . . Teresa?"

"Don't know that sister. Conchita says your pa is mighty ill and won't last much longer."

Slocum fell into step beside Valenzuela as they made their way slowly toward the cell block.

"She sent you?"

"We're going to have to break out. She said your lawyer couldn't get clemency from the governor so you could be with your pa."

"Durant is such a *pendejo*. How long?"

"Conchita said he had a week or two at the outside."

"No, no, how long before we break out? You have a plan?"

"Everybody tells me nobody gets out, yet I'm in here impersonating somebody and they never caught on. The security might be as lax as the way they bring in prisoners."

"Who are you?"

"Call me . . ." Slocum's voice trailed off as they neared the huge man who had pointed out Valenzuela to him. "Call me John. Don't call me by the name I used to get inside."

"You took the place of another to free me? So I could escape and see my papa?" Valenzuela stared at Slocum, openmouthed. "You are not my amigo, yet you would do this for me, a stranger?" Then he burst out laughing. "You are the *novio* of my darling Conchita! You do this for loving her!"

"Keep your voice down," Slocum said.

"Oh, this is *bueno, muy bueno.*"

"Jarvis, you and him got off to a good start," the huge prisoner said, scowling. "You know him from the outside?"

"Jarvis, eh?" Valenzuela nodded sagely.

"What's goin' on?" The prisoner stepped in front of them, blocking their way to the cells, blocking most of the sun as well. "I thought you was gonna have a cow when I said I wanted to beat Jasper Jarvis to a bloody pulp. You *are* a relative of his?"

"Oh, no, Big Mike, he—"

"Shut your trap, Meskin. I ain't talkin' to you."

"I'm not looking for a fight," Slocum said. He rubbed his left hand over the spot where his cross-draw holster usually hung. He felt naked without his Colt Navy and how especially vulnerable he was now. They were drawing a small crowd. The last thing he wanted was to attract attention, and now he was the center of it.

"You some lily-liver like Jasper Jarvis? He always run when it came to a fight."

"Fight! Fight!" The chant went up, and Slocum knew he couldn't walk away.

"Look, it's this way . . ." He stepped a little closer, then launched a kick aimed at the big man's crotch. Slocum's aim was an inch off, and he caught a heavily muscled inner thigh. The impact hurt his knee and sent him stumbling back. And then he was engulfed in two hundred and fifty pounds of smelly, fighting convict.

Slocum blocked a hard punch that would have taken off his head, then another intended to kill him. He danced back favoring his knee, sized up his opponent, faked another kick to the balls, then caught the man's overreaction by driving his fist straight for his belly. Slocum felt the shock all the way up into his shoulder. Every part of this Goliath was oak-hard. Breath whooshed from the man's lungs, then he took a step back and sat down hard, his face beet red as he gasped for air.

Slocum had been in enough fights to know it wasn't over. He judged distances again and launched another kick. The toe of his boot caught the man square on the chin and snapped his head back. This time when the convict flopped onto his back, he was out like a light.

"You, get back, get back!" Guards pushed their way through the circle of prisoners and roughly grabbed Slocum by the arms. "No fightin' allowed. You're goin' into the hole for a week."

Two guards half dragged Slocum away as the sergeant who had checked him into San Quentin came running up.

"You got it under control? You dumb apes. Don't let 'em fight. You know better, and if I catch you bettin' on 'em again . . ."

"Aw, Sarge, we stopped it."

"Let me enter this onto his record. Fighting. Jasper Jarvis, five days in the hole for fighting."

As Slocum was dragged away, he saw the man he had knocked out shaking his head, then become alert when he heard the name *Jasper Jarvis*. Slocum felt the beady eyes boring a hole into his back all the way into the cell block, then down stone stairs and into the dungeon.

He had lied his way into San Quentin to rescue José Valenzuela, and now it looked as if he would spend the next two years serving the sentence of a man he didn't even know.

Slocum cursed himself and Conchita, her brother, and the man he had knocked out, then started all over again on himself.

2

Slocum shivered in the cold, dark cell. He could reach out and touch the stone walls—it didn't matter where he sat in the cell. Worse, there was no light. The pitch-black robbed him of all sense of how long he had been imprisoned there. It might have been minutes, or it could have been hours. His belly growled from lack of food, and his tongue felt like a bale of cotton, all puffy and sticky from lack of water.

But the cold was worst of all. He tried standing, but the ceiling was a few inches too low to allow him to stretch upright. He found the splintery wooden door and tried to pick away at the weakest part, hoping to see out. Too many others had tried and failed. Slocum reckoned they had been locked up here longer than he ever would be.

He settled down with his back against the door since this promised him more warmth—or less cold—than any other position. His head dropped forward and rested on his upraised knees as he dozed. For an instant or an hour? He didn't know, but there came a sharp rap at the door. He felt it in his spine as well as hearing it.

"Get on back away from the door or you'll get shot," came a muffled voice that was strangely familiar.

He did as he was told and the door creaked open to reveal the prisoner he had ridden into San Quentin with standing in the corridor outside, a tin plate and cup in hand.

"Here's yer vittles," Doc said. "Won't get more 'n this for another day, so don't let the rats beat you to it."

Doc handed him the plate, only to be rebuked by the guard behind him.

"None of that. No contact with him. None."

Doc was roughly yanked back and the door slammed shut, but Slocum sat for a moment, his finger holding firmly against the tin plate a slip of paper Doc had passed him. How he was ever going to read in the dark was a poser until he slid the paper away and found a lucifer glued to the bottom of the plate.

He was torn between lighting the match and reading the note and eating. His hunger won out. He wolfed down the stale bread and almost gagged on the tough meat on the plate with it. He hoarded the water jealously in the cup, then couldn't restrain himself. He downed it with a single long gulp that did nothing to soothe the thirst or the way his tongue had swelled.

Still, the food and drops of water restored him and sparked his anger at the guards and San Quentin and . . .

Who else? He tried to blame Conchita and her brother for his predicament, but he had volunteered. Over the years he had learned the lesson not to let nether regions of his anatomy think for him—and this time he had ignored that sage experience. That José might be busted out of this prison was one thing, but doing it was proving more difficult. Slocum didn't know how long José and Conchita's father had before he upped and died, but the lovely, dark-tressed, fiery woman had hinted that it wasn't too long.

Only when he had licked the plate and made certain
not a drop of water remained did Slocum turn back to the
scrap of paper and the solitary match. He would have to
read quick. The match wouldn't last more than a handful
of seconds. Over and over in his mind he played through
how he had to act, where to hold the paper, the match,
how he would read. He finally decided to spread the note
on the floor and use both hands to steady the match. The
initial flare would blind him. He had to keep his eyes shut
and only peer out a little.

So many details. But Slocum had plenty of time. He
pressed his ear against the door, listening hard for any hint
of movement outside. It might be day or night, the guards
might patrol or simply lock a door leading down into the
dungeons. Being caught by a guard took on less urgency
than the need to read the note *now*. What could Doc possibly have thought worth risking ending up down in solitary to pass to him?

Another few minutes' preparation allowed Slocum to
press out the note on the stone floor, then clutch the lucifer. He closed his eyes, struck the match on stone, saw the
dazzling flare through his eyelids, then opened his eyes
fast before the match burned down.

The note was upside down. He hastily spun it around
and scanned it. Doc, for all his boasting of being educated,
could hardly spell, but he had written a considerable
amount on the small piece of yellow foolscap. Slocum
yelped when the lucifer burned down to his callused fingers. He would have traded an inch of his thumb and index
finger to keep the guttering light for even a minute longer.

But the smell of burnt flesh and the blisters on his fingers were all he got.

A smile crossed his lips. He had singed his fingers but
had read through the note and now had something to bol-
ster his spirits. He reached out, pressed his palm into the
wooden door, then worked his way to his right, going to

the wall. From the spot where the walls met the floor, he carefully searched until he found one stone that stuck out more than the others on either side. His strong fingers pried the stone free.

"*¿Quién está?*" came the immediate question.

Slocum flopped belly down on the cold floor and pressed his face close to the hole leading into the next cell.

"My name's . . . Jarvis," he said, almost forgetting his alias.

"*Gringo.*" The word came out as an insult, but the disgust and loss of hope along with it spoke volumes more.

"I'm here to break out José Valenzuela," Slocum said. He saw no reason to lie to whoever occupied the next cell. He needed allies and had to take the risk.

"So? I am not this Valenzuela. I am Procipio Murrieta, the son of Joaquin Murrieta. For no reason other than my proud heritage have they imprisoned me."

"I've heard of Murrieta," Slocum said. "A while back."

"He is dead. I seek only to live peaceably."

"This isn't the place to do it," Slocum pointed out. "Will you help in an escape?"

There was a long silence.

Then, "They will keep those who try and fail in these hellhole cells for years. I am only here for another day."

Slocum pulled back from the small tunnel through the wall and reflected on spending the rest of his life in this cell. Better to be dead. He wanted nothing more than to see the sun again—and hold his Colt in his hand.

"Better to die than suffer them doing to you as they see fit. You said you were innocent. How can you be worse off?"

Murrieta took a while responding.

"I often have this thought. Another year or death? I would choose death."

"Who else is down here? In the dungeon?"

"I do not know. I have tried to speak to whoever is in the cell on the other side, but no one answers. The one who was there might be gone." Murrieta paused, then added, "Or dead."

"If he's dead, can you get to his food and water?" Slocum wasn't the kind to let an opportunity slip through his fingers, but the question brought a hearty laugh from Murrieta.

"You have a sense of humor. I like that, *gringo.*"

"How hard is it to get over the wall?"

"Not possible, but there is another way. I worked on a repair of the wall and saw how badly a section was built. There might have been a doorway there at one time, but no longer. With a pick we can open the way through the wall to the outside."

"How hard will it be opening the way?" Slocum asked.

"It will require many men for it and must be done quickly. The guards patrol constantly. We would have no longer than fifteen minutes."

"The guards would see the hole, wouldn't they?"

"No plan is without risk. San Quentin was not built to be so easily left."

"With Valenzuela and another, can four of us open the hole?"

"Four, yes."

Slocum and Murrieta continued to hone their escape plans. Along with José Valenzuela, Slocum thought Doc would be willing to help. He had risked much to put the two prisoners in contact. The only reason Slocum could think of Doc doing that was a desire to escape himself.

After a while Slocum found himself drifting off to sleep. Time was measured by Doc bringing food once a day, but he had no more notes. Slocum didn't care. Being told where to find the hole and talking to Murrieta made the first effort on the other prisoner's part worthwhile. Slocum felt he owed Doc for that. And since the man was willing to risk so much, Doc was the likeliest to be the fourth needed to escape through Murrieta's wall breach.

"Come on out. Yer time's up."

Slocum shielded his eyes with his arm and peered at the guard in the corridor. The dim light was hardly enough for an owl to hunt by, but for him it was blinding. He got to his feet and staggered out. Going without exercise for almost a week had left him weak. It would take a spell to get his strength back for the escape.

In the corridor he saw two guards waiting, hands on truncheons. The next cell over was already open. Procipio Murrieta had been released days earlier. Slocum tried to step lively but found himself half carried up the steps into real sunlight. He screwed his eyes closed and only slowly opened them to look around the yard, where dozens of inmates milled about. Exercise time was almost over.

"Time to put you back into your cell."

Slocum recoiled from the guard. He wasn't going back into that dungeon.

The guard laughed harshly and said, "Not in the hole. Your cell. Your regular one."

"Jarvis hasn't been assigned a regular cell. He got in trouble right away," said the sergeant, who still carried his ledger. Slocum wanted to cram it down the man's throat until he choked on it. "Put him in with Doc."

Slocum started to complain, then subsided. He let the guard lead him away, acting sullen, but inside he rejoiced. He wanted to learn more about the man who had been his only friend so far within San Quentin's walls.

The cell had two pallets on the floor, almost touching. The straw ticking spilled out of one. Doc sat on the other. He looked up when the guard shoved Slocum inside and slammed the iron-barred door shut behind him.

"You got through solitary," Doc said in a low voice. "You don't look none the worse fer the stint."

Slocum dropped to the unoccupied pallet and leaned back against the stone wall. It was as cold above ground as it was in the subterranean cell. He glanced out the bars and waited to be sure the guard had moved on.

"He's got a bottle down in the office. He ain't likely to be back 'til it's time to let us out for dinner."

"How do you know your way around?" Slocum asked.

Doc laughed harshly.

"Been a regular here for years. Hardly get free and they send me back. I heard about the loose stone in the wall last time I was in. My roommate worked it free on one of his vacations down below. I ain't never been in the cellar myself, 'cept to carry food."

Slocum thanked him for the note and the match, then asked, "Why'd you do it?"

"I seen right from the start you're not the kind what stays locked up. You got a look about you, lean, nasty, not the type to put up with more 'n a week or two of conditions like these."

Slocum worked his way into telling Doc about what Murrieta had said about the hole in the outer wall, finally getting him to agree to join the escape.

"I been locked up too much of my life. I get away, I'm leaving San Francisco and goin' east. Maybe lose myself in Indian Territory. I was born somewhere 'round there, though I don't remember much of it. Might be my pa was a soldier at Fort Gibson." Doc shrugged. "Then again, he mighta been locked up in the stockade and my ma was a Cherokee squaw. It was a long time back."

"We have to take Valenzuela with us."

"That gent you was talkin' with when Mick picked the fight?"

"Mick?"

"Leon Mickleson. Ugly son of a bitch. Most folks inside the walls got more brains in their pinky than he does in his whole danged body, and that's bein' real unkind since most prisoners are dumb as rocks." Doc looked hard at Slocum. "That's something else I seen in you. You're smart. Might not be book smart, but you're always thinkin' and 'less I miss my guess, you come out on top more often than not."

"I'm in here," Slocum said with some disdain.

"There's a real big story 'bout that," Doc said. "I'd bet on it."

"Why do you say that?"

"Jarvis ain't yer name. When the guards call you that, it takes a second for you to remember that's what you're bein' called now." Doc snorted. "Fact is, like Mick, I knew Jarvis. Dumber even than Mick, he was. Now there might be two Jasper Jarvises in the world, but I don't believe in coincidences."

"How do I get in touch with José Valenzuela?"

Doc laughed so hard Slocum wondered what was wrong. Doc wiped tears from his eyes and pointed at him. When he finally caught his breath from the laughter, he pointed at the wall behind Slocum.

"Look for a loose stone. He's in the next cell."

Slocum took a few minutes to find this stone, then pulled it out so he could peer into the next cell.

"Go on, give him a holler," Doc said. "He ain't got company in there. It takes time fer the warden to get in new inmates 'cuz a passel of residents been paroled."

Slocum called out to José.

"Ah, the *novio*," Valenzuela said, laughing. "You have come for me? Am I supposed to claw my way out or will you do the work for me?"

His attitude irritated Slocum, especially after spending five miserable days in a dark hole nestled up against the cell block's foundations.

"If we can get out, there's a way through the wall. It'll take four of us."

"Four?"

"We'll need a pick or pry bar," Slocum said.

"That is easy. I know where the tools are kept. When I go on work detail, I will hide a pick. The guards never check," Valenzuela said. "When will we make this escape?"

Slocum mumbled. He hadn't gotten that far yet in his planning. He didn't even know how they were going to get free of their individual cells.

"Doc, the one with you, he knows where this hole is?"

"Murrieta does. He'll be the fourth one."

"Procipio Murrieta? You have fallen in with desperate company, hombre."

"We can get with him tomorrow in the exercise yard," Slocum said. He motioned Doc to silence when the man started hissing.

Then he looked over his shoulder and saw a guard staring at him, tapping his truncheon against his left palm in a slow, thoughtful way.

3

"What's goin' on?" the guard asked. He rattled the bars in the cell door with his truncheon.

"I'll tell you what's goin' on," Doc said, jumping to his feet and going to the cell door. He interposed himself between the guard and Slocum, who quickly replaced the stone from the wall. "He went buggy down in the hole. He's talkin' to the damned wall! I won't put up with it. Gimme another roommate! I demand to talk to Warden Harriman. Get him the hell out of here. He might be dangerous!"

The guard laughed, shook his head, and moved on, never once looking back at Slocum or asking about the hole in the wall.

"He didn't see the hole," Slocum said, sitting back and heaving a deep sigh.

"He prob'ly did. But I gave him somethin' else to think on. Always gets a laugh when I say it might be dangerous locked up with whoever's in the cell." Doc hung out the cell door and looked around the cell block, then he laughed.

"This place is chock-full of dangerous gents, and most of 'em are in guard's uniforms."

Slocum thanked his lucky stars that Doc understood the system and how to deal with the guards.

"You think Valenzuela next door knows where to find the tools we'll need?" Doc asked.

"I'm more worried about Murrieta finding the hole through the outer wall," Slocum admitted.

"You got a point, Jarvis—or whatever your name is. We're gonna be hangin' out there all exposed, no matter where the hole is. If it takes more 'n a few minutes to open it up, we're gonna hang. Or wish they'd hang us since spendin' the rest of our lives down below in that dark hell is worse than anything else they can do."

Doc turned, flopped onto the pallet, tucked his hands under the back of his head, and stared up at the ceiling.

"Git some sleep. We're gonna need it real soon."

"Why's that?" Slocum asked.

"You wouldn't know, but it'll be dark of the moon tomorrow night. If we don't try it then, we got to wait another month."

Slocum sucked in his breath as he stretched out on the hard pallet. He had lost all track of time being in solitary. He hoped that Conchita was still waiting for him and José's pa hadn't up and died.

Slocum, Murrieta, and Valenzuela huddled together near the wall. The warm sun beat down on them. The canvas prison uniform would have been uncomfortable, but Slocum was so glad to see the sun again he didn't complain.

"Been working the far side of the yard, in the garden," Valenzuela said. "I have hidden a pick there." He hardly moved his lips as he spoke. He didn't look at either Slocum or Murrieta and might have been doing nothing more than enjoying the sunlight.

"That is good," Murrieta said. "It is near where the wall was patched."

"How do we get out tonight?" Slocum asked.

Both men laughed at him.

"The one in the cell with you—Doc—he will show you. It is not so hard," Valenzuela said. He sighed. "I would again see my lovely Conchita."

"And your pa. Your sister said he could hang on until you got to him."

"Ah, yes, his deathbed," Valenzuela said. "You are a good man to do this for *su novia*."

Slocum moved away without answering because a pair of guards began drifting in his direction. He wanted to keep as much distance between him and the blue-uniformed men as possible. The less he had to do with them, the better chance he had to stay out of solitary.

Then he saw the problem rising up in front of him and tried to veer away. Mick wasn't having any of it.

"You!" the huge man bellowed. "I got a bone to pick with you!"

Slocum knew any confrontation with the enraged inmate would land them both in solitary again. He doubted Valenzuela and Murrieta would wait another month to escape now that he had gotten them together, matching the tool with a plugged way out through the wall.

A quick look around showed he was in big trouble. Three guards, including the sergeant with his ledger book tucked under his arm, were all homing in on him, hawks with the pigeon reflected in their eyes. Slocum saw no way of avoiding the angry inmate. He wasn't afraid of Mick but was of being tossed into solitary again.

"I don't want to fight," Slocum said, but he would if it came to that. Better to knock this stupid son of a bitch down again and end up in solitary than to crawl. There'd be another chance for him to escape from San Quentin, though he had no idea when or what it would be.

There would be plenty of time to think up something if he had to waste away for a week or two in the dark, cold subterranean cell.

Slocum balled his fists, judged the distance as the bull of a man charged toward him, and then simply stared when Mick fell facedown in the dirt. His feet kicked feebly, and he tried to get to his hands and knees. He didn't make it because Doc swung a rock he clutched in his hand again and caught Mick behind his ear a second time. Blood gushed from the double cuts.

"Take that! You can't say a thing like that. You can't insult me no way, no how!" Doc turned and held up the bloody rock as the guards swerved from circling Slocum and went to him.

"You know better 'n to hit a man from behind, Doc," the sergeant said, flipping open the book. The guard scanned the pages, turning them quickly. He finally looked up. "It was last time you were in that you got into trouble. But it was for gambling. What happened, Doc? You want to spend the rest of your life behind these walls?"

"He cheated me, Sergeant Wilkinson," Doc said, trying to kick a still unconscious Mick. The guards pulled him away. He began cursing and kicking, trying to get free to continue his assault on a man three times his weight and half again his height. As the guards took him away, Doc craned around, stared squarely at Slocum, and winked broadly.

"You old fool," Slocum muttered under his breath. But he wasn't going to pass up the chance Doc had given him.

Only he was in almost as big a mess as if he had been dragged off to solitary. Valenzuela had told him that Doc would help get him free that night so the four of them could escape. That there were three now wasn't the problem. Doc's knowledge of how to get free of the cell when the time came was.

Four guards picked up Mick and lugged him to solitary. Slocum heaved a sigh of relief at that. The ornery hunk of gristle would be out of his hair for a spell. With any kind of luck, Slocum would be on the other side of the towering prison walls by the time Mick got free.

He felt a touch of admiration for Doc, then knew the old geezer's life would be shortened. Mick wasn't the kind to let a sneak attack go unanswered.

The bell rang, warning him that exercise time was over. He walked deliberately toward the cell block, his mind racing. There had to be something he could do to get free that night. What skills did Doc have that he didn't? What knowledge of the prison and its system? As he pushed through a door, scraping against another inmate whose sleeve had caught on a nail head protruding from the doorjamb, an idea came to him. He wasn't sure that this was what Doc would have done, but it was all he could think of.

Every step of the way to his cell, Slocum worried at the cuff of his canvas uniform, pulling a thread free and rolling it up into a ball. Part of the canvas had come away. He added this to the ball and smeared dirt and grease from his fingers on the thread.

"Inside, Jarvis," a guard said, shoving him forward when he hesitated.

"I can't go in again. I can't!"

The guard shoved again. Slocum caught himself against the edge of the door and jammed the ball of thread into the latch, hiding what he did with his body. Before the guard could use his truncheon to move him inside, Slocum swung around and stepped into the cell on his own. The door slammed shut, iron ringing from the force used by the guard to close it.

Slocum grabbed the bars and held on to keep the door from swinging back out. He had listened hard and knew what the guard didn't. The thread had prevented the door from latching properly. The guard grunted and moved on to Valenzuela's cell to be sure the door was secured. Slocum wrapped his arms around the bars and used his weight to hold the iron-barred door shut until the guards had left.

Carefully releasing his death grip, fearing he might have caused the door to lock in spite of the way he had jammed it, Slocum watched the door swing open a few inches. He caught it but held tight until a dark form moved in front of his cell.

"You are free?" Valenzuela pressed close. "I cannot open the door for you."

Slocum let the cell door swing wide.

"Bueno," Valenzuela said. "We are to meet Murrieta in the garden."

"You sure the pickax is still there?"

Valenzuela shrugged eloquently.

"If it is not, we use our fingernails to claw through."

"Can we do this with only three?"

"We must dig faster, perhaps not be so stealthy." Valenzuela moved like a ghost past the cells. Slocum worried that a prisoner might see them and shout out an alarm. Two guards played cards at a table near the door leading out to the exercise yard. The guttering candle on the table between them hardly lit the table, much less the area where they slipped through shadows.

Slocum grabbed Valenzuela by the arm and pointed. Valenzuela shook his head and pointed to a doorway some distance from the card-playing guards. They reached the door without either guard noticing. Valenzuela rattled the door handle a few times, then sprung the flimsy lock. He slipped inside, Slocum pressing close behind.

"There. We go down," Valenzuela said. "I have seen storage cellars. From there we can get out of this building."

Slocum doubted it would be that easy, but to his surprise it was. They passed through the storage room, found a window leading up to ground level, and wiggled through it, coming out only a dozen yards from the inmates' vegetable garden. The scent of growing things caused Slocum's nostrils to flare. It had been too long since he'd had such earthy aroma in his nose. The musty, solitary cell had been suffocating in its closeness, and the larger cell with Doc had been hardly better.

The wind fitfully caused waist-high plants to sway gently. Slocum considered how he might take cover in the vegetation if a guard came by. The rows were far enough apart that he might be seen, but the dark of the moon gave added benefit to anyone trying not to be seen.

"There, up on the wall," Valenzuela said, pointing.

Slocum saw a guard walking slowly by. His silhouette was indistinct, but he seemed to be carrying a rifle in the crook of his left arm. There was no way to tell what he was looking at, but he continued along the catwalk, turned a distant corner, and vanished from sight. Slocum let out a breath he hadn't even known he was holding.

"Where's the pick?"

"At the end of this row," Valenzuela said. "Where is Murrieta?"

"Here," came the soft voice.

Slocum jumped. He had not heard Procipio Murrieta come up behind them, and that worried him. He had thought he was alert. Murrieta might have moved like an Apache, but that was no excuse for Slocum to be such a greenhorn.

"See the dark spot on the wall? That is where they patched."

Slocum made out the faint outline of a doorway. The stone wall had been breached here, probably with a gate intended for supplies to be taken to the prison kitchen nearby.

"They closed it a year ago to better watch what comes into the prison," Murrieta said.

"And to keep prisoners from going out," Slocum said. He moved like a shadow crossing another shadow and went to the wall. He pressed his fingers into the cold stone and felt the plaster seam marking the doorway outline. Valenzuela joined him, Murrieta right behind.

"Where is the fourth?" Murrieta asked.

Slocum shrugged off an explanation. He was more interested in getting the hell out of San Quentin. Once free, he became John Slocum again, and Jasper Jarvis was a thing of the past. For his part, it couldn't happen soon enough.

His fingers found a bit of loose plaster. He tugged and a section came free. Beneath the plaster lay a thick stratum of concrete.

"Let me," Valenzuela said, shouldering Slocum aside. He swung the pick he had retrieved and sent a hunk flying from the plug. Slocum grabbed it and carried it to the garden, putting it in one row. Murrieta followed with a second piece, but the sound of Valenzuela working echoed like cannonade.

"Keep it down," Slocum cautioned. He looked up at the walls but didn't see the patrolling guard.

"Got to get through. We only have minutes before the ground patrol comes."

Valenzuela worked furiously, prying loose even larger hunks of concrete for Murrieta and Slocum to lug off and hide. The sound of the pick point hitting wood caused Slocum to look around.

"Getting close," Valenzuela said, panting from his exertion.

"I'll take over," Slocum offered. He took the pick from the man's hands and applied his own expert strokes to the door, tearing out hunks of half-rotted wood. The other two men kept the area behind him free of betraying debris. The feel changed suddenly when the point of the pick penetrated to the far side of the door. Slocum put his foot against the wall and heaved. A section of door came free, letting a gust of air from the other side of the wall blast through.

Slocum inhaled deeply. The air was no different from that inside San Quentin's walls, but it smelled sweeter than any perfume. It carried the scent of freedom.

Murrieta hissed, and Slocum heard the other two men rushing for cover in the garden. He turned and saw a guard round the far corner of the building holding most of the cells and head toward him. From the rhythmic sound of wood against flesh, he knew the guard slapped his truncheon against his palm the way he had seen San Francisco Specials do it as they patrolled the worst section of the Barbary Coast.

Slocum gripped the handle of the pickax and considered fighting the guard, then discarded the idea immediately. Any ruckus within the walls would draw attention. He took a step to follow Murrieta and Valenzuela into the dubious refuge provided by the garden plants, then stopped. He could never make it without being seen.

He pressed himself back into the cavity he had carved in the wooden door and felt it yield behind him. He dug his heels in and pushed as hard as he could. The hinges yielded although the door didn't give way. He sucked in his gut and held his breath as the guard came closer. The man stopped, looked around, then worked to build himself a smoke. His face was momentarily illuminated in the flare of the lucifer lighting the tip of the cigarette. Slocum recognized the guard as the one who had peered into the cell when he had first talked with Valenzuela. He wasn't as sharp as a whip, but that didn't mean he couldn't send Slocum and his two partners to the hell of solitary if he saw anything amiss.

The guard puffed contentedly on his cigarette, not moving.

Slocum continued to push hard against the door, hoping

to get it open so he could reach the other side of the wall. The guard wasn't armed so he couldn't shoot Slocum if he had to run, but sounding the alarm would bring a swarm of guards Slocum wanted to avoid.

The guard finished his smoke, then walked toward Slocum. The guard stopped, shuffled his feet in the dirt as if noticing a hunk of concrete or something else out of the ordinary. He gave a slight shrug, as if realizing he couldn't figure out what he had seen, then continued his patrol. Slocum remained flattened in the cavity in the wall. The moonless night worked in his favor and hid him enough so that the guard walked past.

It took another interminable minute before the guard reached the far end of the building, then turned and disappeared. Slocum wasted no time spinning around and hammering the pick against the hinges. They popped open within seconds. A swift kick sent the door tumbling away.

Both Valenzuela and Murrieta joined him.

"Well done, *novio*," Valenzuela congratulated him. He laughed in a way that irrationally irritated Slocum. He didn't like being reminded that Conchita considered him her lover, although it was true. "She will reward you well."

"*Silencio*," Murrieta said. He pushed them through the open doorway. "We must not betray ourselves now."

Slocum agreed with the son of Joaquin Murrieta. The less said now, the better.

They had come out on the west side of the prison. San Francisco Bay lapped on the shoreline to their left, giving them a constant beacon so they wouldn't be distracted from their escape and walk in circles. In the darkness Slocum knew this was a distinct possibility. The last thing he wanted was to end up where they had started. The only way off the outjut of land into the Bay was westward. Then they might swing around and get down to Tiburon and take the ferry across to Oakland. Better to go farther south still and find a way across the

Golden Gate to San Francisco, if that ferry wasn't running at night.

He stopped and stared at their striped canvas prison garb and knew that wouldn't happen until they changed clothes. The wooded area thinned as they ran farther west.

"I need to get my bearings," Slocum said.

"What for? We can go only this way. In any other we would have to swim," said Murrieta.

"I cached some clothes and guns," he said.

"What?" Murrieta stopped and stared at Slocum.

"Why would you do such a thing unless . . ."

"Unless he got into prison to break me out," José Valenzuela said proudly. "Conchita did not find a fool for this dangerous jailbreak."

"You were sent?" Murrieta shook his head in disbelief. "I have planned for months how to escape but never did I have anyone outside helping me."

"You didn't need it," Slocum said, slapping him on the back. "You had me. I've got clothes for me and José."

"Conchita raided my wardrobe, eh?" Valenzuela laughed heartily. "I must see how she chose to dress me."

Slocum stared at Valenzuela but could not see the man's face in the dark. Something about the way he spoke of his sister put Slocum on edge.

"They are after us," Murrieta said, turning to look at their back trail.

"I hear nothing," Valenzuela said. "Come, let us keep going, find those clothes Jarvis has told us of." He reached out, made his hand into a gun, and pretended to fire. "I would also have a six-shooter in my hand once more. You have a six-shooter for me?"

Slocum ignored Valenzuela and went to stand beside Murrieta. The wind blowing through the trees masked much of the sound. What wasn't robbed by the wind was swallowed by the sound of waves, but Slocum heard a single yelp from a dog.

"Bloodhounds," he said.

"They found the hole sooner than I thought they would," Murrieta said. "We should have taken more time and hidden the doorway better."

Slocum knew they should have done a lot of things differently, but there hadn't been time. He had drawn an ace when Doc stopped Mick from taking a swing at him. But the dark of the moon had dictated escape tonight or waiting for a month. They might have been successful escaping during a storm, but the drought had spread north. Thunderstorms were a rarity at this time of year.

"We didn't have a choice," Slocum said. He looked around for some way to cover their scent. He had hoped to find a stream or other river. He suspected the closest river that would have been useful hiding their escape lay miles to the north. The Petaluma River might as well have been in Kansas for all the good it did them.

"Can we make it to the shoreline?" he asked.

"It is too far, but that is the only way to throw off the dogs," Murrieta said.

"They come closer!" José Valenzuela heard the baying dogs for the first time. "What are we to do?"

"Due south," Slocum said, trying to get the lay of the land squared away in his head. They might be a mile away. If they hurried, there was a chance—slim—of staying out of the clutches of the guards so eagerly pursuing them.

"They are angling toward the Bay," Murrieta said. "They will find us before we can get a boat or swim away."

"There is no way to swim," Valenzuela said sharply. "The water is too cold. And there are sharks!"

"I will lead them away," Murrieta said. "You go to your dying father," Murrieta said to Valenzuela.

"You can't—" Slocum started.

"What can they do to me they have not done before?"

"I'll get you out," Slocum promised.

Valenzuela laughed harshly, and Procipio Murrieta

grabbed Slocum's hand and shook it. Then he hurried straight south.

"Come on," Slocum said. "He's buying us some time, but it won't be much."

He headed back westward. He had left clothing and weapons at the junction of the road leading to San Quentin and the road working its way north toward Oregon. He longed to get on a horse and see what the lovely Pacific Northwest had to offer after the dry California countryside—and its prison.

4

Slocum dug like a gopher, kicking up a cloud of dirt and leaves as he hunted for the package he had left at the cross-roads. The darkness didn't help, but he had been cagey enough to hide the clothing and six-shooters near a distinctive rock beside the road.

"Hurry, they are coming. I feel it in my bones."

Slocum looked up from his digging and saw Valenzuela silhouetted against the starlit sky. The man looked nothing like his sister, but Slocum wasn't going to pry. There might have been different mothers. Childbirth was a dangerous undertaking, although the Valenzuelas seemed to live well and could probably afford a decent midwife. Still, life was uncertain, and he had no idea about how rich the family really was. All he knew was that he had helped Conchita when her carriage had broken down, and one thing led to another.

That had been almost three weeks ago. The pressure of time and getting José back to see their father before the old man died weighed heavily on him. If he hadn't gotten into the fight with Mick on that first day, they might have escaped earlier. As he returned to unearthing the oilcloth-wrapped package, Slocum realized that he was belittling himself for no reason. The escape had occurred because of a half-dozen small things. Doc had sacrificed his chance to escape so that the other three could make it to freedom. Murrieta had similarly given Slocum and Valenzuela the gift of escape by diverting the guards chasing them.

He wondered about the son of California's most famous outlaw. It hardly seemed possible Procipio Murrieta was guilty of anything, but Slocum had known some cold-blooded killers in his day who were sweet as brown sugar until someone crossed them. The little contact he'd had with Murrieta hinted that this wasn't the way the man was, but he had been sent to San Quentin for a reason.

Slocum snorted, wiped dirt from his eyes, and went back to digging. Hell, he had been inside the prison, and he hadn't committed any crime. A slow smile came to his lips. He had done his share of thieving and robbing and even killing when necessary, but nothing that would have qualified him for such a grim penitentiary. The smile faded when he realized he might have been hanged if the law caught up with him and twigged to the fact he was a judge killer.

After the war, he had returned to Slocum's Stand in Calhoun, Georgia, wanting nothing more than to recuperate from his wounds and begin farming again. His ma and pa were long dead, and his brother Robert had died at Pickett's Charge. He had lost himself in work until a carpetbagger judge had trumped up a phony tax lien and had ridden out with a gunman to seize the property.

He had gotten the property—a grave down by the springhouse. His gun slick had been buried a few feet lower on the hill, and John Slocum had ridden out, followed by a warrant for his arrest. Killing a judge, even a Reconstruction thief of a judge, was a federal crime.

But Slocum doubted any lawman in the San Francisco

area had seen that wanted poster. All anyone inside San Quentin knew was that he was Jasper Jarvis.

His fingers closed on the buried package. He tugged, got the parcel out, and quickly opened it. His clothes and Colt Navy were safely inside. He shucked off his canvas uniform, wanting to get rid of the striped outfit as quick as he could.

"There, she chose well," Valenzuela said, reaching over Slocum's shoulder to hold up a fancy embroidered shirt. It was gaudy and would attract attention. Slocum started to say something, then stopped. Perhaps this was for the best. Let José mouth off and make a spectacle of himself. That might be the last person a marshal would look at.

He quickly pulled on his jeans and stood brushing off dirt that speckled his shirt and Stetson. Only when he was sure he was clean enough to pass casual muster did he strap on the cross-draw holster and settle his six-gun in it.

Valenzuela looked at him, his eyes went wide, then narrowed.

"You wear that like a man accustomed to using it," he said, pointing at Slocum's ebony-handled pistol.

"There wasn't any way I could leave horses. We've still got a posse on our trail."

"A posse?" Valenzuela laughed. "You sound like an outlaw. Inside, I thought you to be . . ."

"What?" Slocum turned and squared off.

Valenzuela shrugged and said, a smile curling his lips, "*Un pata cojo*. I was wrong. I must commend Conchita on her choice in men when we see her. She has told you where to meet?"

"I have no idea where to find her other than in your house where your pa's dying," Slocum said. The pitch black hid Valenzuela's reaction, but Slocum thought the man recoiled at this. "You know how we can get horses?"

"We are across the Bay from San Francisco," Valenzuela said. "We must cross the Golden Gate. Or we could go north, circle until we get to Oakland, and take that ferry. They did not place San Quentin where it was convenient for any who dared escape."

Slocum listened hard for the sound of pursuit but heard only the sounds of night and the distant lapping of waves.

"To the Bay," he said. "We can find a boat that'll take us across." He didn't want to leave a trail. Stealing horses suited him, but not now. The owner would complain to the law, and it wouldn't take much imagination on the part of any of the San Quentin guards to know the thieves were their escaped prisoners.

"They might not know who has escaped," Valenzuela said.

It was Slocum's turn to smile. They thought Jasper Jarvis had broken out. Then he realized that he could tell them he was John Slocum until he was blue in the face, and it wouldn't matter. They cared less about the man than the crime he committed. As John Slocum, he wasn't supposed to be in prison, but they saw only a ledger entry. Slocum imagined Sergeant Wilkinson running his stubby, ink-stained finger down a column of names and matching the phony name he found with the very real face of the man he had checked into the prison.

"Let's get the hell out of here." Slocum started walking just off the road. The shoulder was smooth enough so he wouldn't stumble on many rocks in the dark, but being away from the middle of the road gave him the chance to dive for cover if he heard the search party coming. As he walked, he kept an inventory of places to hide, spots where he might hole up and shoot it out. No matter what, he wasn't going back into that prison.

After an hour hiking, they came to the shoreline. In the distance he saw San Francisco. Gaslights burned brightly on either side of a dead black area—the Barbary Coast. That blight on the city held the toughest gangs, the most dangerous outlaws, the worst of the worst. If necessary,

Slocum could disappear into that city within a city, but he preferred to travel through the town to the south part of the city itself where Conchita waited with her dying father.

If the old man hadn't already kicked the bucket. From all the lovely woman had said, he was close to opening death's door when Slocum agreed to get José out of San Quentin. It had been ten long days, and a great deal could happen in that span when you were nearly dead. Slocum wished he had seen the old man to get a better idea of his condition, but Conchita had insisted her pa remain in a dark room and not be disturbed. All Slocum had heard were asthmatic wheezing and occasional moans.

Slocum scratched bug bites he had received while in the solitary confinement cell, then reached out and grabbed Valenzuela by the arm. To his credit, the man did not cry out but instead looked to where Slocum pointed.

Two men sat on rocks, bent over as they concentrated on some hidden chore. Nearby they had secured a rowboat that would serve nicely to cross the Golden Gate to the city.

"We should kill them," Valenzuela whispered. "They will notify the prison if we do not."

Slocum wasn't averse to killing when his life depended on it, but these two fishermen didn't deserve such a fate just because they owned a boat he wanted to use.

"Let me talk to them," Slocum said. "Come quick if you hear gunfire."

"But—"

Slocum gave Valenzuela no chance to argue. He strode forward confidently, sure he could deal with a pair of men who dragged fish out of the Bay. A few yards away, he stopped. The men were heavily armed. He saw shotguns resting against the rocks where they worked to repair a rope. Both had knives in their hands, and he was sure they had pistols jammed into their belts. They were armed to the teeth.

"Law's on its way," Slocum called. Both men grabbed for their shotguns.

"Who're you?" demanded one of the men. Whatever they were, *fishermen* didn't describe their occupation.

"A gent only a few minutes ahead of a big posse. They're after . . . smugglers," Slocum said, taking a guess at what the men were up to. From the way they poked their shotguns in his direction, he knew he had hit the nail on the head. What they might be smuggling was beyond him, but it hardly mattered if he could get them to do what he wanted.

"Who tipped 'em off?" The second smuggler was more composed. Slocum took him to be the leader.

Addressing him, Slocum said, "Doesn't much matter. We've got to get across the water, back to the city."

"We?" The leader laughed harshly. "How are you dealin' yourself into this game?"

"Four men rowing will get us across the Bay faster than just two."

"Four?" The leader understood what Slocum meant, whirled, and found himself staring down the barrel of Valenzuela's six-gun.

"I can shoot them both," Valenzuela said.

"Four of us rowing'll make better time," Slocum said. He walked forward and saw six small caskets secured with iron straps in the bottom of boat. "We might have to leave the contraband."

"No!"

"Then you definitely need a couple extra sets of hands on the oars." Slocum let the two smugglers whisper back and forth a few seconds, then pressed his advantage. "We can leave you here with those casks and just take your boat."

"No! We . . . we can all get across. The tide is out. It's dangerous anytime, but in the dead of night it's goin' to be damned near suicidal."

"Then let's get to killing ourselves," Slocum said. He motioned to Valenzuela to join them. For the first time, he was glad Valenzuela was with him, watching his back, making the right play and doing it without a lot of lead flying. The sound of gunfire might draw the prison guards. By now they must have reached the shoreline some distance along the coast closer to San Quentin.

"You ain't gonna rob us?"

"We're honest crooks. All we want to do is stay ahead of the law," Slocum said with enough sincerity that the two men both nodded at the same time. They climbed into the boat and took their places on the bench seat while the one Slocum pegged as the boss pushed them off. He got them into the choppy water, then dropped the frayed end of the bowline to the bottom.

That explained what they were doing. Without the line, it wasn't possible to tie up the boat at a dock. On this rocky beach, they had simply pulled the boat far enough onto land and didn't have to secure it otherwise.

"We take turns. You two start," the head smuggler said.

"I have a better idea," Slocum countered. "My friend and you row, then we switch off. That way somebody's always watching to be sure nothing goes wrong."

The smuggler thought about it a moment, then agreed. Slocum sat in the stern while the other smuggler took the prow. His boss and Valenzuela took the oars and began rowing.

The Bay proved even choppier than Slocum had anticipated, and by the time they reached the far side, avoiding the curious eyes of soldiers at Fort Point, he was sick to his stomach from the bouncing motion. He thought Valenzuela would make some snide comment about how shaky he was when he climbed onto a low dock at North

Beach, but Valenzuela was as wobbly-legged as he was.

"Good luck," Slocum said to the smugglers.

"We had that already, if we really avoided the law," the boss said. He reached for his shotgun but didn't pick it up. "Did we?" he called.

"Did we get away from the law?" Slocum asked. "We sure as hell did."

The smuggler relaxed. Slocum had told him what he wanted to know.

"We should have killed them both," Valenzuela complained when they were out of the smugglers' earshot. "They will ask about a reward. The guards will lie, we will be back behind bars before the sun comes up."

"I don't think so," Slocum said. "I don't know what they were carrying in those barrels, but they're not going to the law. Not about us. They want to keep as much distance as we do from anyone wearing a badge."

Valenzuela grumbled, but Slocum ignored him. He was too busy looking for a means to speed them along their way to the Valenzuelas' house south of town. He slowed and then stopped when he saw a man shoved out of a carriage hitting the cobblestones hard. He stirred drunkenly on the pavement but didn't show any other signs of life. The man who had struck him shifted over to the middle of the hard seat in the buggy and started to snap the reins, but one had fallen down in front.

Slocum moved quickly, got beside the horse, and soothed it, then snared the errant rein and held it out to the thief.

"Here you are. You should be more careful, dropping it like that."

The man was shabbily dressed and looked like a drowned wharf rat. He reached for the rein in Slocum's hand like a striking snake. Slocum was quicker. He caught the thief's wrist and yanked so hard the small man became airborne and fell heavily to the pavement beside his victim.

"I'll cut you!" the thief cried, coming to his feet with a foot-long blade in his hand. The gaslight glinted off the wicked tip as he advanced.

Slocum gauged distances, then swung the rein still in his hand like a whip. The leather strap lashed the thief in the face. As he recoiled from the pain caused by the welt on his cheek, Slocum snapped the rein back, caught the wrist with the knife, and yanked hard.

The thief was no knife-fighting novice. He adroitly changed hands, his left now holding the knife. But he stopped when he found himself staring down the barrel of Slocum's six-shooter.

"You don't hafta shoot," the thief said.

"See if your friend has any cash on him," Slocum said, his eyes darting to the drunk and then back.

"Naw, he's tapped out. Me and him been drinkin' half the night. Took him forever to get that soused."

Slocum hated sneak thieves but said nothing. He kept the six-gun pointed at the man's face until he backed off. With a flourish, the man returned the knife to whatever hidden sheath it had been drawn from, then backed off, hands up and palms facing Slocum.

Slocum waited until the man turned and ran before lowering his pistol.

"Get in," he told Valenzuela. "It's not much but it's better than hoofing it."

"Not so much," Valenzuela said uneasily. He held his head canted to one side as he listened. In the distance Slocum heard police whistles. "We might do better to leave it if the police are after him."

Slocum knew the drunk on the ground might have committed some vile crime, possibly being too free with his money, and that had drawn the Specials. They traveled in packs like feral dogs and wouldn't be satisfied until they were adequately paid off or had killed someone.

With a quick turn, Slocum got into the buggy and

snapped the reins. The swaybacked horse snorted and began pulling.

"Wait, wait for me!" Valenzuela jumped aboard as Slocum pulled away. "You would not leave me! Not after you saved me from the prison. What would *su novia* say if you returned without me?"

Slocum didn't have an answer for that. He wasn't all that sure anymore what Conchita would say when he showed up with her brother.

He snapped the reins again and brought the horse to a canter to get the hell away from the policemen appearing like ghosts out of the fog at the far end of the street. Having a shoot-out with a platoon of them was the last thing he wanted.

He wasn't too sure what the first thing he wanted was, though. He would just have to find out when he delivered José Valenzuela to his dying father's bedside.

5

"I cannot wait to see her," José Valenzuela said as they approached his home. He was shifting so much on the buggy seat that Slocum worried the carriage would tip over. Valenzuela swung out far and stared ahead. The sun was just creeping up and sent long shadows slanting toward them. Slocum had the feeling of driving into the sunset rather than into the rising sun of a bright new day.

Valenzuela jumped out and hit the ground running, disappearing into the front door without breaking stride. Slocum took a few minutes to drive the rig around back so it would be out of sight. The house was not far from the main road going north into San Francisco, and he didn't want a casual passerby to see the buggy or the horse. Chances were slim anyone would recognize the horse and buggy as being stolen from a drunk in northern San Francisco, but he took no chances. Memory of the San Quentin walls rising around him turned him wary. To return there was not in the cards.

He went around and stood in the low doorway to see Conchita and José clinging to one another. As he went into the small house, they parted. Conchita looked flustered, and José looked like the fox that had just eaten the chicken. All he needed were feathers around his mouth.

"You see your pa?" Slocum asked pointedly.

"I was on my way. He is very ill and still sleeps. I took a moment to thank my sister for being so clever to get you to break me out of prison." José stepped behind Conchita, who stood a little stiffer for a moment, then José went into the bedroom just off the main room.

"Oh, John, you did it!" Conchita rushed into his arms and smothered him with kisses that made the jailbreak and everything he had endured seem worthwhile.

"Did he make it in time?"

She pushed away and looked at him, puzzled.

"Your pa. He's still aware of things around him?"

"Oh, yes, there is great pain, but he is not in a coma. José came in time."

"How much longer do you think he has?"

"Papa?" Conchita laid her cheek on his chest. He felt her heart beating in her breast and smelled the perfume of her long, dark hair. She clung fiercely to him. "Not so long, but he wanted to see José. You have done a great thing, John. A boon. A favor that can never be repaid."

"I'd like to look in on them. To see how they're doing," Slocum said, moving to push Conchita out of the way. He heard strange sounds from the tiny room where José had gone.

"Let Papa enjoy José's jokes," she said, gripping him harder. "He could always make Papa laugh. It is good for both of them."

"I won't be a second," Slocum said, not sure why the laughter bothered him so. That Conchita had verified it was laughter made him certain he wasn't imagining things.

"I know you won't, John," she said, her hand pressing hotly into his chest, holding him where he stood. The hand worked slowly downward until it cupped his crotch.

She began squeezing gently, then pressed her palm into the growing bulge.

She turned her beautiful face up to him, closed her ebony eyes, and pursed her lips, waiting. She didn't wait long. Slocum had gone through hell for this moment. He kissed her. She returned the passion with more ardor than he could have hoped for. Her body moved against his and her legs parted so she could wrap her thighs around his upper leg. Conchita began moving up and down, like a cat rubbing against a table leg.

She broke away breathlessly, then stood on tiptoe and licked along the line of Slocum's stubbled chin until she got back to his earlobe. She nibbled gently and whispered, "Outside. To the shed in back. It is ready for you—for us!"

Conchita pulled him behind her like a child pulling along a wagon. Slocum had to duck fast or he would have hit his head on the lintel as they went out into the morning sun. It felt hot and fine against his face. He felt renewed and happy that he had been able to help the Valenzuelas.

"Hurry, hurry, race you!" she cried. As Conchita dashed away from him, she began shucking off her clothing. Her blouse was the first to land on the ground. She stumbled and spun and got off one shoe and then the other before she reached the shed. For a moment, she fumbled with the latch. Then she had the door open and stood outlined by the doorframe.

Conchita dropped her shoes inside and began moving her shoulder sinuously to work out of her undergarment. Slocum had picked up her blouse but now slowed to watch the show she put on for him. A final shimmy brought the camisole down around her waist. She stood gloriously bare to the waist. Slocum caught his breath at the sight of those apple-sized breasts, each capped with a brown circle. In the middle of those targets grew hard little nubs betraying her arousal.

"You like what you see, my hero?" Conchita spun

about, then bent over and hiked her skirt. She wasn't wearing anything under it.

Slocum had gotten so hard watching her that he felt pain in his crotch. He began unbuttoning his fly as he went to the doorway, where she waggled her bare butt in his direction. He sighed as the final button popped open, and he snapped out, fully erect. Two quick steps took him to the curvy ass presented to him. He put his hand on the sleek, warm flesh and felt the woman quivering.

"Yes, John, yes," she whispered. Conchita reached out and grabbed the top of a crate stored in the shed. Her stance widened, inviting him to do more from behind.

Slocum stepped up to do his duty. He felt the warm half-moons on either side of him, and then he moved lower. The plum tip of his manhood touched her nether lips. He felt the moisture leaking from her. She wanted him as much as he wanted her. He had gone through hell for her, and this was his reward. Part of it.

His hips levered forwarded, and he sank an inch into her heated core. He paused, relishing the feel roiling up into his groin. He was becoming fully alive now. His hardness turned to steel and began to ache with real need.

He lightly spanked her mahogany-hued butt and heard her delighted yelp. He reached around her waist and pulled her back powerfully. For a moment he thought he would pass out. The tightness around him, the heat, the slickness, all worked on his senses. His loins blazed hotter than any prairie fire. When she began rotating her hips and stirred him about deep within her, he knew he couldn't simply stand still to fully enjoy this delight.

He began stroking with sharp, quick strokes. Friction mounted between her inner walls and his fleshy stalk. He gripped her hips even more firmly, and they fell into a rhythm, crushing together, stimulating one another, getting the most out of this carnal coupling as they could. When it felt as if he would explode within her like a stick of dynamite, Slocum slowed the frantic pace and caught his breath.

"No, no, don't stop. Oh!"

He reached up and caught at her dangling breasts. Firm in his hands, they barely overflowed each of his palms. He had big hands, but Conchita was ample enough to give him something to work with. He squeezed and stroked and finally caught the brown nubbins between thumbs and forefingers. Rolling the nips around brought cries of even more intense joy to her lips.

And then he started driving his fleshy spike back into her. Caught between the two regions of stimulation, Conchita went wild with need. This spurred Slocum on until there was no holding back. The fierce tide rose within him and edged upward, burning and giving intense pleasure until he erupted within the tightness she so avidly offered him.

He heard her cry out as she shoved her rump back into the circle of his body. She shivered and shook and cried out again, then sagged forward, catching herself on the edge of the crate until he slid limply from her heated interior.

"You are so good, John, so very good." Conchita turned and flaunted her breasts, cupping them and offering them up to him. He couldn't resist such a treat. He bent, suckled first on one and then the other. She gasped with the sudden intrusion of his middle finger into her tightness again. Between his oral ministrations on her teats and his delving finger, he got her off again. This time she staggered back and perched on the edge of the crate. Her face was flushed and her eyes wild with lust.

"Never have I found such a lover. Not even . . ."

"Not even who?" Slocum asked. "I want to know my competition."

"There is no one who can compete with you, John. You are perfect. Absolutely perfect." She threw herself forward.

Her arms circled him and pulled him close. Slocum wasn't going to complain but thought something was wrong. She purred like a contented kitten, and he certainly had no complaints, but something wasn't right and he couldn't figure out what it might be.

"We'd better get back and see how your brother and pa are getting on."

"Why? José can do well on his own. You should know. Was he not capable helping in his own escape?"

Slocum had nothing to say about that. Both Doc and Murrieta had sacrificed themselves for him and Valenzuela to escape. Valenzuela had contributed little and would have brought down the guards if Slocum hadn't convinced him to keep a low profile rather than shooting anyone who moved. Valenzuela was a hothead and had ended up in San Quentin for a reason.

Still, Slocum had ridden with worse in his day. Bloody Bill Anderson and his commander, William Quantrill, had been conscienceless killers. Anyone wearing a blue uniform was fair game, no matter their age. That had gotten Slocum gut-shot and left for dead when he refused to kill Yankee sympathizers in Lawrence, Kansas, who were as young as eight years old. But compared with the killers serving with Quantrill's Raiders, José Valenzuela was a babe in arms.

"Something's wrong," Slocum said. The uneasy feeling grew. "Where're the horses kept?"

"On the other side of the house, but do not worry about that, John. Come, let us—"

Slocum shook his head as he drew his six-shooter. Something felt wrong. He had survived during the war by listening to this inner voice. Sometimes it whispered; other times it screamed. Slocum was almost deafened by it now.

With Conchita trailing behind, struggling to get her blouse pulled up over her shapely shoulders, Slocum rounded the house and saw the crude corral.

Empty.

"José's gone," he said.

"There is nothing to worry about. He will be back soon. I know it."

Slocum ignored her and went to the house. He pushed open the front door with the toe of his boot, then edged into the dim interior. Calling out wasn't too smart; Slocum went to the bedroom door where the elder Valenzuela had been on his deathbed.

Had been.

The room was empty. The bed was neatly made and might not have been slept in recently.

"Both José and your pa're gone," he said. Slocum turned to face Conchita, who stood with a curious expression on her face. It was a mixture of anger and confusion. "Where'd they go?"

"I . . . I cannot say. Perhaps José took him to a doctor. Our father. To a doctor."

"Why'd he do something like that if the old man was dying? The time's past for giving him a tonic or some other medicine."

"José knows so much more than I do, than our papa does. He might have seen and known the right place to go."

"You're lying. Where are they?"

"You cannot call me a liar! I will not stand for it. You get out. Now. *¡Con veloz!*"

"So I get your brother out of San Quentin and you run me off?" Slocum reckoned he had gotten paid out in the shed, and there had been so many times prior to him agreeing to carry out her crackbrained scheme, but it hardly made up for a week in solitary confinement in the bowels of the prison. He had been tricked before and likely would be again, but he felt angrier at himself for letting this pretty *muchacha* dupe him so easily.

Rather than leaving as he was told, Slocum went into

the bedroom and began rummaging about. He had no idea what he was hunting for. There wouldn't be any money to recompense him for all he'd been through, but he wanted more to find something that would tell him where José and his father had gone. They had left almost immediately after Conchita had lured him out to the shed, so they had been planning something. He wanted to know what it was.

"Get out!" Conchita cried. "You cannot rob us!"

"Wasn't planning on that. I want to know what you and your family are up to." He found a small metal box. Using the butt of his pistol, he knocked off the small lock and dumped the contents onto the bed. A few coins and a sheaf of papers comprised the entire contents. He left the coins and pawed through the papers. There were maps and scribbles in Spanish that he didn't understand.

"Tell me what this means," he said, holding out one map for Conchita, but she had disappeared. He stuffed the paper into his pocket and strode into the main room. The sound of a horse got him moving outside in a rush. He saw Conchita riding bareback on the horse that had so reluctantly pulled the buggy. He took a couple steps in her direction, but the dust cloud obscured her direction when she got to the nearby road.

He took off his hat and slapped it a couple times against his leg to dislodge some of the dust. Then he began walking, fuming as he went. He hadn't even come out of this ridiculous failure with a horse, even a swaybacked nag hardly up to carriage duty.

Slocum reached the road, looked once in the direction of San Francisco, and began walking the other way. There was nothing for him to the north. For that matter, he knew there was nothing southward either. He had come this way to escape the heat and drought and saw no reason to return to it. Mostly, he needed to find a horse so he could range due east, circle around San Francisco Bay on the Oakland side, and then ride as hard as he could for the Pacific Northwest. Oregon had to hold better circumstances.

Barely had he gone a mile when he heard the thunder of hooves behind him on the road. Whoever rode down on him was in a powerful hurry. He considered stepping aside and seeing who was intent on killing his horse under him, then got the prickly feeling at the back of his neck that he ought not indulge this curiosity. He left the road and went to a dry acequia. The drought here wasn't as bad as down south, but it was enough to make the irrigation ditch little more than a mud puddle.

He slipped over the edge and flopped down, waiting.

The riders approached, then slowed, and finally stopped about the place he had left the road.

Sunlight glinted off badges pinned on the riders' vests. He slid his Colt Navy from his holster when one of the lawmen pointed to the tracks he had left, then slowly traced along his trail to where he hid in the irrigation ditch.

Slocum knew he was in for trouble when the posse dismounted, fanned out, and started toward him.

6

"You lift that iron and you're a dead man," shouted the man Slocum took to be the leader. "Boys, get ready to shoot. He don't look like he's the surrendering kind."

A quick glance left and right confirmed Slocum's worst fears. He was already caught in a cross fire. The deputies on either flank had a clean shot at him. He might take out one, but the other would ventilate him in the span of a heartbeat. And that didn't even take into account the two gunmen flanking the leader. One held a rifle like he knew how to use it, and the other's grip was steady on his six-shooter.

"Don't get itchy trigger fingers," Slocum said, holding up his hands. He felt exposed and about ready to die. All it would take was a single deputy to get a tic, and lead would fly.

"Come on over here, and keep your hands up in the clouds. I swear, we'll shoot if you don't!"

As Slocum got closer to the lawman, he saw a sheriff's badge.

"Look, Sheriff, I—"

"Shut your face," the lawman snapped. He snared Slocum's six-gun and tossed it to the nearest deputy. Even then, the sheriff kept a keen eye on Slocum's every move.

"He matches the description, Sheriff Bernard."

"What description?" Slocum asked. He got a pistol barrel laid up alongside his head. He felt all the strength go out of his legs as he collapsed to his knees. The world spun in crazy circles, and pain filled his head.

"Don't go doin' that, George," Sheriff Bernard snapped. "He done surrendered. It's up to us to keep him that way until the trial."

"You reckon he's got a price on his head? Other than for the robbery?"

Slocum didn't know which of the deputies asked the question. He went cold inside.

"My horse died. I was just going to—"

"Get him in irons," the sheriff said. "And if he keeps yammering like that, gag him."

Slocum felt cold metal cuffs snapped around his wrists. He was yanked to his feet and shoved along to the road. A rope was looped around the chains holding his wrists together. The ends were fastened around a deputy's saddle horn, then they all turned their horses' faces and started back north toward San Francisco.

If the drunk identified him as the one who stole his horse and buggy, Slocum knew they might just string him up. Stories of vigilance committees were rife in San Francisco. But the sheriff seemed one of the rarities, a peace officer who actually enforced the law and didn't permit his prisoners to be mistreated. Or at least Slocum hoped that was true of Sheriff Bernard.

To his surprise, they didn't follow the main road back into San Francisco but took one angling off west toward the ocean. Slocum heaved a sigh of relief at this. The longer he stayed away from where the prison guards might hunt—in San Francisco, most likely—the better his chances of getting away. Whatever the posse thought he had done, he could alibi his way out. After all, he had been in the area only a few hours. Conchita would sweet-talk them.

Or would she? They hadn't parted on the best of terms, and he had no idea what her brother and father had been up to. They had hightailed it from the house in a big hurry once José had returned.

Slocum slogged along, keeping up the pace the best he could. If he flagged, he suspected he would be dragged along and wasn't sure Bernard would much care about that. The sheriff and two deputies rode some distance ahead, chattering like magpies.

Footsore and about ready to collapse after making it through a low pass and to a level spot where he could see the Pacific Ocean, Slocum considered trying to engage the deputy so intent on keeping him moving in some conversation. The more he found out, the more improved were his chances of getting away.

It would be better if he could talk his way out of whatever the sheriff thought he had done.

"What town's that? Down on the coast?"

"Miramar," the deputy answered before he realized he wasn't supposed to talk to the prisoner. "Shut up. No yammering."

"Whatever you think I did, I didn't. Never been to Miramar. Didn't even know the name." Slocum slipped and slid down the steep road, pebbles causing him to stumble repeatedly.

"Shut up."

Slocum found it almost impossible to talk and keep up when the rider put his heels to his horse's flanks and picked up the pace. By the time they arrived at the tiny jail on the outskirts of town, Slocum was half past dead.

"Inside," the deputy ordered. He jerked hard on the rope, and Slocum fell facedown in the dirt.

"None of that, Jess," the sheriff warned. "We want him presentable when he goes up in front of the judge."

"Damned stinkin' bank robber."

"Bank robber?" Slocum looked up in wonder. "I haven't robbed any bank. Why do you think I have?"

"Witness. She saw you galloping like the wind, carrying the canvas bank bag filled with the gold coins."

"She?" Slocum knew who this witness was.

"On the road not a couple miles from where we nabbed you. Right pretty young thing, she was."

"If I was riding, where's the horse? Where's the money?"

"Now, those are matters we're going to determine," Bernard said. "Get him inside, boys."

Strong hands dragged Slocum into the jail, his toes dragging in the dirt. They threw him into one of two cells before removing the shackles on his wrists. He rubbed where the iron had chafed the skin raw and bloody. He hardly winced when the sheriff slammed the cell door with a loud clang and turned the key in the lock.

"Find the money," Bernard ordered his posse. "He musta hid it somewhere along the road. It wasn't more 'n a mile or two between where we caught him and the spot where the girl saw him."

"She was a real looker, even if she was a Mexican," said a deputy.

"Git your worthless asses out there and find the money. Hez Galworthy'll have a conniption fit if you don't."

"Think he'll give us a reward if we find the money?"

"Hez is like most bankers. Tighter 'n a snake's asshole when it comes to money, but he just might. Now git!"

The deputies left. The sheriff heaved a sigh and sank down behind his desk. It had been positioned so he could stare into the cells, leaving his back to the doorway.

"Tell me about the robbery," Slocum said. "How many men robbed Galworthy?"

"You know, it might just be that something different 'n

I thought happened out there on the road. There were two of you. Might be you had a falling-out. Your partner take the money and your horse? You might as well come clean, especially if he double-crossed you. What do you owe him anyway?"

Slocum considered his options. He might confess to being a bank robber just to implicate José Valenzuela. He had no doubt at all that José had been the robber, and that his sister had been the one who had put the posse on Slocum's tail. But if he did that, he might get revenge on Valenzuela but would also end up in jail for years.

The memory of San Quentin caused him to set his jaw in determination not to return there as a prisoner. He owed Valenzuela. He would deliver justice himself—at the muzzle of his six-shooter.

"We got witnesses enough to know your partner's some old geezer."

Slocum's mouth fell open. He snapped it shut and tried to put on a poker face. He wasn't sure how well he succeeded since the sheriff watched him like a hawk. Barely had José Valenzuela returned when he and his pa had ridden out to rob the Miramar bank. The elder Valenzuela hadn't been near death at all. Conchita had duped him into believing her pa was dying, but all she wanted was for the old man and José to get back to what was likely their profession: robbing banks.

"You have other robberies done by the same two men?" Slocum asked.

"I haven't looked, but that's a mighty good idea. I might convict you of more 'n one in the area. Of course, the money from them's likely to be gone, isn't it? Otherwise, why would you be so brazen about committing a daylight robbery?"

"Anyone shot?"

"Now, you know the answer to that. Lot of lead flyin' 'round but nobody was hit. Scared the hell out of old Hez.

Probably the most excited he's been in years." Bernard laughed and shook his head. "You'd have to see his wife to appreciate that. I swear, she's uglier than a mud fence."

Bernard kept shaking his head and chuckling as he opened a drawer in his desk, took out a stack of wanted posters, and began leafing through them. Slocum considered distracting the sheriff but knew that wouldn't work. Aching from so much walking, he dropped back on the cot and stretched out, staring at the ceiling. Bits of concrete had come loose, exposing iron bars. Some were rusty, but it would take hours to scrape through them, and he knew Bernard would never allow that much work.

Slocum closed his eyes intending to only rest for a moment, he came awake with a start when he heard a loud argument getting more intense. He sat up and saw a blue-uniformed back between him and the sheriff. His heart almost exploded when the man turned slightly to expose sergeant's stripes.

"He's mine. He's an escaped prisoner by the name of Jasper Jarvis."

"Now that may be, Sergeant Wilkinson, but he's my prisoner right now. You can have him after the trial. I got him fair and square for bank robbery."

"He's a prisoner what belongs in San Quentin since that's where he was when he busted out."

"Do tell," Sheriff Bernard said dryly.

"You don't believe me. I don't like any man callin' me a damn liar."

"Never said you were lying, Sergeant. Just saying he's staying put until he stands trial. That might add on years to his sentence. What was he in for? You called him Jarvis?"

"He'll be in for five more escapin' the way he did. Him 'n three others. We caught one of them right away. The other got away, prob'ly with Jarvis."

"Mighty interesting and irrelevant," Bernard said, his voice hardening. "He's my prisoner right now."

Slocum had never wanted to be in a county lockup as badly as he did now. If Wilkinson prevailed, he would not only be back in San Quentin, he'd be in the hole again. The dark. The cold. The isolation.

"I can git me a San Francisco judge to issue the order," Wilkinson said.

"Be my guest. That'll take you a few days, if you can sober one up that fast to scribble his name. By then we'll have this varmint indicted and on the docket to stand trial. The local justice of the peace is a man devoted to his community. That means he knows robbing the Miramar bank takes precedence over returning him to San Quentin."

Wilkinson pounded both quart-jar-sized fists on the sheriff's desk so hard the desk jumped off the floor to crash back down.

"You ain't listenin' to me, Sheriff."

"Can't help but listen, you talking so loud. Why don't you get on out of here and find that other prisoner you lost? This here Jasper Jarvis isn't going anywhere."

For a moment Slocum thought Wilkinson was going to hit the sheriff, then he saw how Bernard sat at his desk. If the prison guard had moved a muscle and tried to touch the lawman, he would have gotten a bullet to the belly. The sergeant grunted and left, growling like a grizzly as he went. Only then did Bernard stick his six-gun back into its holster.

"You know some mighty unpleasant people, Jarvis."

"Name's not Jarvis," Slocum said.

"Doesn't matter. Sergeant Wilkinson there thinks it is."

"He's wrong. And you're wrong about me robbing that bank."

"That's the beauty of the law. I don't have to be right.

If a jury convicts you, it doesn't matter what I think. I might be wrong about you and Hez's bank. Won't be the first time I made a mistake, if I am. But I don't think so. There was no reason for that pretty girl to put me on your trail the way she did unless she saw what she said she did."

"Might be she was in on the bank robbery," Slocum said, testing the water with the truth.

"She wasn't the man who did the actual robbery and she sure as hell wasn't the old man waiting with the horses to make the getaway. I know a hawk from a handsaw, and I know a curvy señorita from a man all crippled up with arthritis." Bernard laughed. "I'm getting a better class of liars these days. You, at least, can make me laugh when you proclaim your innocence. Most of 'em I throw in that cell don't even try to alibi themselves."

Slocum knew when to give up. He was digging his own grave and had to find another way out of this jail. If it came down to a trial, he might get away from the bank robbery charges but would never convince the authorities that Sergeant Wilkinson shouldn't be given back an escaped prisoner.

He slowly studied the bars, the floor, the walls, everything in the cell without finding a possible way out. The iron had rusted but would require too much noisy work to break through. That left the lock since he saw no way to pry off the hinge pins on the cell door.

Slocum felt a growing anger at himself for getting into this predicament. He should never have agreed to such a cockamamie idea as breaking José Valenzuela out of San Quentin, much less letting Conchita dupe him so thoroughly.

"Dying pa," he snorted.

"What's that?" Sheriff Bernard looked up from the book he was reading.

"Nothing," Slocum said. "Just thinking out loud."

"Not speaking to you." The sheriff turned his book upside down on the desk to mark his place and reached for his six-shooter. The door slammed open and caught Bernard's arm, knocking him off balance. The six-gun went skittering off the desk and hit the floor. The hammer crashed down on a cartridge and sent a slug ricocheting around the small jailhouse.

Slocum was on his feet, hanging on to the bars. A masked man surged in and slugged the sheriff. Bernard collapsed across his desk. It took a few seconds for the masked man to find the keys to the cell, but Slocum wasn't cheering him on.

"You don't think much of letting the law take its course, do you, Wilkinson?" Slocum asked. The San Quentin guard pulled down the mask and sneered.

"I think it ought to, which is why I'm takin' you straight on back where you belong, Jarvis. This hick sheriff ain't gonna prevent justice from happenin'. You might just waltz on out of his courtroom, and they would never bother tellin' me."

Slocum backed up when Wilkinson motioned him away from the cell door with his six-shooter. He waited for the opening that might come when the guard got the key in the lock. There would be an instant when Wilkinson would be distracted. And there was.

The prison guard looked down when the key refused to turn easily. The lock finally snapped open with a metallic clang. Slocum launched himself at the same instant, hitting the door with his shoulder and driving it back into Wilkinson. The pistol went off. Slocum felt its hot breath across his cheek but ignored the sting. He lashed out with his fist and caught Wilkinson on the side of the head, further driving him away. Losing his own balance, Slocum fell atop the guard. His knee crushed down into the man's belly.

"Jailbreak!"

The cry startled Slocum. Sheriff Bernard had come to and fumbled in his desk drawer for another gun. Slocum rolled, came to his knees, and slammed his palm hard against the desk drawer, smashing the sheriff's hand. Bernard cried out, this time in pain.

A quick yank opened the drawer. Slocum grabbed his Colt Navy and stumbled to his feet. On his way out he pulled his gun belt from a peg and tumbled out into the warm California night. The lack of moon hid him within a few yards. He ducked down low, darted for cover, and worked to strap on his gun belt as he ran.

Behind him in the jailhouse came several gunshots. Wilkinson and Bernard were shooting at each other. Slocum hoped both lawmen were good shots.

He plunged into the sultry night, wanting as much distance between himself and the Miramar jail as possible.

7

Slocum settled down to catch his breath. He needed a horse if he wanted to get the hell out of the clutches of two different lawmen. At least he considered the San Quentin guard as a lawman. Wilkinson obviously had the authority to take an escaped prisoner back to the prison without going through the court.

Thoughts of San Quentin made Slocum simmer and almost come to a boil. How Conchita had duped him! All she wanted was her brother's release so he and their father could go on a bank-robbing spree. He had thought he might actually love her, but her words had been lies even as her body spoke to his. Slocum tried not to get involved like that. Thinking always worked better for him in the long run than responding emotionally, but Conchita had been different. He thought she had been different.

He sat up a little straighter when he heard the steady clop-clop of a horse's hooves against the dry ground. At this time of night it wasn't likely to be a traveler. He dived off the main road, and this part of the countryside showed no sign of cultivation or mining. Nobody homesteaded here so the only rider was likely to be Wilkinson or Sheriff Bernard.

He slid his six-shooter from his holster, glad that he had grabbed it from the sheriff's drawer. Fighting either of the lawmen with his bare hands wouldn't have kept him from jail.

Poking his head up, Slocum chanced a look toward the road and saw the dark silhouette of a big man astride a horse. From the movement in the darkness, he knew the rider was tracking him. It was damned near impossible without a light, but the sudden flare of a lucifer so the rider could see the ground and Slocum's track also revealed Wilkinson's ugly face.

Slocum leveled his six-gun and sighted in. He considered simply shooting the prison sergeant but didn't squeeze down on the trigger, fearing Wilkinson might have brought the sheriff along with him. The gunfire as he escaped the Miramar jailhouse made it unlikely the two had thrown in together, but Slocum couldn't tell. He didn't want a murder rap added to all the rest of the charges against him.

A rueful smile curled his lips. If he killed Wilkinson, that would be the only crime for which he'd be truly responsible. The rest were trumped up or lies concocted to get him into San Quentin. He wasn't Jasper Jarvis, and he sure as hell hadn't robbed a bank. Not in these parts, and not recently.

For a moment, this got him thinking in different directions. If the Valenzuelas had the bank money, robbing them would be easier than stealing from the bank itself. He deserved something for all they had done to him. Then he realized Conchita's lies had stung him worst of all. He didn't like being played for a fool.

Wilkinson's horse neighed and drew Slocum's attention back to the prison guard. The bulky man bent low, still in the saddle, and lit a second match. Whatever he saw pleased him because he snuffed out the match quickly and sat straight in the saddle. Again Slocum considered pulling the trigger, but in the dark the shot was difficult. The range worried him, too. If he had a rifle, he might have attempted shooting the horse out from under Wilkinson.

The guard rode straight for where Slocum hid.

From the way Wilkinson advanced, he didn't know how close he was to his quarry. This settled the matter for Slocum. He twisted about, crouched down behind the log where he had taken his respite, then waited. The horse passed close to him, snorting and trying to turn at the smell of the man Wilkinson hunted.

Sergeant Wilkinson jerked hard on the reins to keep the horse moving straight ahead. "Don't go gettin' skittish on me. We're close. I know it." Wilkinson reached down to pat the horse's neck.

Slocum moved like lightning. He stood and grabbed, both hands circling Wilkinson's brawny wrist. Digging in his heels, Slocum yanked with all his might. In spite of Wilkinson's bulk, the prison guard went flying through the air. Slocum never released his hold on the sinewy wrist. Instead, he jerked upward and felt the arm separate from the shoulder. The dislocation left Wilkinson with only one good arm—even better, he landed hard and lay stunned.

Following up his initial attack, Slocum swung around and fell heavily, his knee driving into Wilkinson's belly. The air gusted out in a sudden *whoosh!* Slocum pulled his pistol, swung hard, and caught Wilkinson alongside the head. The crunch told of a solid impact. The guard slumped, unconscious.

Panting harshly, Slocum rolled Wilkinson over onto his belly and used strips from the man's shirt to hog-tie him. With the guard's pistol stuck into his belt, Slocum stepped back and studied his handiwork. He wasn't satisfied. He added a gag to keep him from crying out. Only then did Slocum go after the guard's horse.

Swinging into the saddle, he turned the horse's face back toward the road and reached the spot where a decision had to be made. North returned him in the direction of the Valenzuelas—and San Quentin. If he went south, he could curl around the bottom of San Francisco Bay and then head north to Oregon. But searching for him as an escaped prisoner might have ranged in that direction from San Quentin. It was better if he returned south and kept riding. From there he could decide what was best, although the thought of the Arizona desert this time of year wasn't too appealing.

On the other hand, having his tongue swell up from lack of water in the Sonoran Desert was more enticing than being sent back to San Quentin.

He rode south.

Dawn cracked the sky and promised an open road where he could make better time, but something settled into the pit of his stomach. He had ridden a half-dozen miles from where he had ambushed Wilkinson. The guard wasn't likely to have followed him, but an uneasy sensation told Slocum somebody was watching him. He rode off the wide dirt track and circled to get a look at his back trail.

Nothing. He was the only one on the road. But the feeling refused to go away. Slocum had learned to listen to this sixth sense because it had kept him alive over the years. He was tired to the bone and knew he should rest. Worse, his horse was beginning to stumble. Riding the horse to complete exhaustion was foolhardy. On foot, he would be an easy target for Wilkinson or Sheriff Bernard.

Thought of the sheriff made Slocum narrow his eyes and study the road where he had just ridden more closely. Did he see a fountain of dust rising? Or was it only a fitful morning breeze? He knew he might be inventing pursuit when there wasn't any. Wilkinson might have shot the sheriff and left him dead in the jailhouse. There had been the exchange of shots that Slocum hadn't bothered to investigate.

He dismounted to let the horse crop at tufts of grass growing between the trees. Stretching betrayed aching muscles. He yawned and knew he would fall over in a stupor if he didn't get some sleep, but he couldn't do that because of the uneasy feeling. Not seeing anyone on his trail ought to have quelled the sensation—but it hadn't. If anything, he felt even jumpier.

Making sure the horse was tethered but still able to pull at the juicy grass, Slocum began hiking through the woods intent on keeping hidden from anyone who might be traveling the road.

Less than a mile along, he was glad he had been so cautious. Three men had left the road and huddled around a small fire heating coffee. He didn't recognize two of them but the third stood, looked around as he drank from a tin cup, and then stretched to reflect a sunbeam off his badge. Sheriff Bernard's instincts were as good as those of Sergeant Wilkinson.

Slocum cursed under his breath. He had a small posse on his tail and wouldn't stand much chance shooting it out with them. Even if he could ambush them the way he had Wilkinson, he would have to risk getting shot himself.

The sheriff finished his coffee, wiped out the cup with his bandanna, and then stashed his gear in his saddlebags. The others broke camp, preparing to follow their escaped prisoner.

Slocum found himself in a predicament. He had walked almost a mile from his horse. The posse could reach the spot where he had left the road long before he could return to his stolen mount. If he hightailed it now, he might mask his trail on foot, but he was sick and tired of walking everywhere.

The sheriff led the way, a deputy riding alongside.

The third deputy was having a difficult time with his saddle. Every time he tried to tighten the belly strap, the horse reared and fought him. Slocum knew this was his chance. Gripping the pistol he had taken from Wilkinson, he walked briskly toward the struggling deputy. The man never looked up from his battle with his horse until it was too late.

Slocum swung the pistol and buffaloed the deputy, dropping him like a stone. The horse shied away and continued to kick up a fuss. Slocum ignored the horse for the moment, more intent on the pistol in his hand. Etched into the barrel were the words PROPERTY OF SAN QUENTIN. He hefted the weapon, then dropped it on the ground and took the deputy's six-shooter. Only then did he turn his attention to the reluctant horse.

More than once in his checkered career, Slocum had worked breaking broncos. This horse hadn't been properly trained and to take the time to do so now would guarantee that he would end up in the sheriff's jail again. Instead of leaping on the saddle, Slocum grabbed the cinch and loosened it. The horse settled down and actually let him get close to yank the saddle from its back. He tossed the gear away, took the reins, and vaulted onto the animal's back. The horse reared and tried to throw him, but its heart wasn't in the fight. Slocum concentrated on simply staying on, then guided the horse away from the fallen deputy and got on the road. He turned northward and let the horse have its head.

When the horse began to tire, he gently guided it toward the wooded area on the eastern side of the road, got into the trees, and began working his way back southward toward the horse he had taken from Wilkinson. This horse didn't much cotton to a rider, but not having the saddle screwed down tight made it an easier ride.

The sheriff and his deputy had ridden a fair distance down the road, but when the third member of their posse hadn't caught up, both had retraced their path. Slocum watched them passing in the direction opposite to his as he threaded his way through the trees. By the time he reached his horse, the one he'd taken from the deputy took it into its head to throw him at the first opportunity.

Slocum slid from the horse's back before that could happen and clung to the reins. He had use for the horse that didn't include riding. It took him a few minutes to go over his mount to be sure it was rested and well fed. He stepped up, looped the other horse's reins around the saddle horn, and then continued his way south through the copse until he reached a wide meadow that stretched flat and inviting—except that any rider on the road would spot him instantly.

It might be a half mile or more across. Slocum had to guess whether the sheriff had found his fallen deputy yet. Probably so. Leaving Wilkinson's pistol might muddy the water a little, but Slocum couldn't count on the sharp lawman being all that confused. By laying the false trail, Slocum gained a little time. Or possibly not. Bernard might decide that he was being decoyed away and split his forces. One deputy might go northward while he continued south. The one on foot might ride with the other deputy.

Slocum rubbed his eyes. He was too tired to think straight. All this "what if" was giving him a headache. What he knew for a fact was he had at least a half mile of wide open meadowland to cross and sitting worrying what the sheriff might do accomplished nothing.

He put his heels to his horse and fell into a quick gait to get to the far side where he could disappear once more into the forested area. The deputy's horse put up something of a fuss, but a constant pull on its reins kept it trailing along without much trouble, though Slocum knew the horse would rear and lash out with its hooves in an effort to break free the instant the pace slackened.

And that was exactly what happened. He slowed as he approached the trees and saw thick undergrowth. The thorny bushes would cut his horses' legs if he pushed through them. Seeing no way around it, he trotted to the road. Where the road had been straight up to this point, it began winding about through the forest. That would give him a measure of cover—only he realized he had no time to gallop far enough to gain it. The sheriff and a deputy appeared a half mile back, just coming to the far edge of the meadow.

Horse at a dead gallop, he raced along the road, but he had tired out both animals. He released the reins on the deputy's horse so it could follow its own head and leave a bogus trail. Slocum doubted the sheriff would be fooled. Worse, the sheriff probably knew Wilkinson had nothing to do with slugging the other deputy if he recognized Slocum. A half mile away, possibly taken by surprise, the sheriff might not have gotten a good look at his quarry.

Slocum had to believe he had. Trying to decoy the sheriff and make him believe Wilkinson had attacked the deputy was a spur-of-the-moment plan. He wasn't any worse off if it didn't work. But that did nothing to get him out of the sheriff's tenacious clutches. The man probably considered an escaped prisoner to be a personal affront. If he recaptured Slocum, he could lord it over Wilkinson, too—if he didn't throw the prison guard in jail for trying to break Slocum out of the Miramar jail.

He took a sharp curve in the road, bent low over his horse, trying to get as much speed as possible. The horse's strength faded again. Slocum felt the energy leaving the legs even as the huge lungs began to strain for air.

The sudden gunshot caused Slocum to jerk around. His heart jumped when he thought Bernard was close enough to open fire on him. But he saw two men step from the forest, one on either side of the road, rifles to their shoulders. They fired at the pursuing lawmen, not Slocum.

His horse stumbled and almost fell, forcing him to regain control. As he slowed, he saw a man step out from the forest, a rifle in his hands. Slocum went for his six-shooter, then stopped.

"This way if you want to get away," Procipio Murrieta said, motioning into the woods.

Slocum put heels to his tired horse's flanks and rocketed in the indicated direction.

8

"You're the last man I ever expected to see," Slocum said, dismounting to stand beside Procipio Murrieta. "That's twice you saved my bacon."

"That is one dangerous man who follows you," Murrieta said.

"You don't have to tell me that. He's sheriff up in Miramar and about as friendly as a wolf with its fangs stuck in my leg."

"This I know. He will never stop. Does he know you as a prisoner from San Quentin?"

"Reckon he does," Slocum said. "Sergeant Wilkinson came by to make sure he knew, but Bernard wouldn't release me. Wilkinson tried to break me out, but I got away."

"The sergeant is again returning to San Quentin," Murrieta said. "The gossip is that he lost his gun and his horse but will not say how."

"I had both. This filly?" Slocum said, patting the neck of the horse. "That's his, and I left his pistol beside a third deputy."

"The other horse you let go free in the woods?" Murrieta laughed heartily. "You are a horse thief, Jarvis."

"Not my name," Slocum said. He introduced himself.

"You hide from a bigger prison sentence?" Murrieta had the look of a man who wanted the truth and would burrow and dig until the wound festered or he found out what he wanted. Slocum told him the sorry story of how he had been duped.

"So your *cojones* did your thinking, eh?" This made Murrieta laugh again. Slocum wasn't as inclined to feel charitable about it now. "That proves you are a man. What man has not been betrayed by a woman?"

"This one won't be again anytime soon," Slocum said. He looked around uneasily. They were only a dozen yards into the woods away from the road. "The sheriff . . ."

"He will not trouble us. Sheriff Bernard is no fool. With only one deputy, he would see he is no match for so many guns."

"Your gang?"

Murrieta snorted and shook his head.

"I am not my father. I am no outlaw by intention. But the law makes me into one. All I want is to raise crops and a family. In peace."

"You were in prison because your pa was an outlaw."

"Whenever a crime is committed, I am the first the sheriff seeks. If I cannot find an alibi, I am arrested. So it is with all those who follow me."

"Follow you?"

"I am *alcalde* for my small village. I try to lead them, to keep order according to our own laws, but it becomes more difficult."

Four men rode up, all sporting bandoliers crammed with shells. They could stand off an entire army with that much ammunition. Slocum decided the sheriff wasn't such a coward after all if he saw even one of Murrieta's band and hightailed it back to town.

But simple *peones* wouldn't be armed to the teeth, even if it was as Murrieta claimed.

"You see their guns, eh? We are no longer pushed about. We fight. I did not ride with my father, but I still learned a great deal about rifles and fighting from him. Come along, Slocum. We go to my village."

Slocum swung into the saddle, happy to put even more distance between himself and Sheriff Bernard. As they rode slowly, he asked, "How'd you get out of San Quentin? After you gave yourself up so Valenzuela and I could get away, I figured you would be clapped into solitary for a year."

"The time to make a good escape is when they least expect it. I returned to their prison, tail between my legs like a whipped cur, and they thought I was defeated. They became careless and I escaped before they had even returned me inside the walls." Murrieta rocked back in his saddle and held out his leg, pulled up his pant leg and showed where the skin had been cruelly abraded. "I got off one leg iron, and the rest was easy."

"But you had to get away from their search parties," Slocum said.

"You wonder if I had a way to freedom and denied it to you and Valenzuela? No," Murrieta said. "Luck favored me. I got to the Bay and found a boat. It leaked, but I rowed hard and found a fog bank. I continued to row, but when the fog lifted, I saw I had rowed back almost to where I had found the boat." He chuckled. "It was then that my strength almost fled, but I refused to surrender. I rowed across the Golden Gate and lost myself in San Francisco. Once there . . ." He shrugged eloquently.

Slocum figured Murrieta had plenty of friends there willing to get him back to his village. They might even have ridden with his father, though Procipio would be hesitant about making that claim since he obviously wanted to be thought of as law-abiding.

Slocum wondered how much of the law Murrieta actually followed as they rode into his town. The adobe buildings were pockmarked from bullets, and the men who came out were all heavily armed. This might be an outlaw hideout rather than a simple farming village. But farther to the east Slocum saw fields of beans growing. Acequias had been built for irrigation, and farm tools were stacked near many houses. Whatever the truth, it was more complicated than casually looking around would ever reveal.

"You are tired. Hungry, too, eh? Come into my house, and we will see to your needs."

Murrieta dropped to the ground. A young boy of ten or twelve rushed out to take the reins. He took Slocum's, too, and led the horses away. The rest of Murrieta's gang had disappeared among the houses. Anyone riding up now would think this was nothing more than a sleepy farming community rather than an armed camp.

Slocum ducked his head low as he entered Murrieta's house. The smell of brewing coffee made his nostrils flare. His belly rumbled loudly enough for Murrieta to hear.

"Sit. We eat simply but well." He dropped a china plate in front of Slocum and ladled out beans. A tortilla was added. Slocum had already wolfed down a mouthful when Murrieta put a cup of coffee near his hand.

"How is it you came to this part of California?" Murrieta asked.

Between mouthfuls, Slocum recounted his travels up from the drought-stricken South. He was feeling more human by the minute. When he'd polished off a second plate of beans and two more tortillas, he was feeling downright sociable.

Movement behind him, though, sent Slocum reaching for his six-shooter. He hesitated when he saw a woman silhouetted in the doorway, the morning sun shining through her dark hair and completely erasing her face. But there was no disguising the curves and the lithe way she moved.

"Lo siento," she said. "I did not mean to startle you."

"I don't usually sit with my back to the door," Slocum said. "Getting careless."

She spoke in rapid Spanish to Murrieta. Slocum followed some of it but not much. There was trouble of some kind between two of the villagers.

"I must go make peace. Maria will keep you company." With that, Murrieta left, pushing past the woman.

For a moment, Maria hesitated, then came in and stood by the table.

"Is there anything more I can give you? It looks as if Procipio has fed you well."

"Not his cooking," Slocum said. "Yours?"

"Oh, no, not mine." Maria looked away and actually blushed.

"But you wish you could cook for him?"

Her fiery eyes fixed on Slocum. This time there was no shyness.

"He is not for me. He is not for any in the village, though he claims there is someone down south. Procipio hints at a family."

"So he doesn't fool around with any of the women in this town?"

"Never!"

Maria pulled up a chair and sat next to Slocum. Their knees brushed. She did not pull away, and he damned himself when he didn't draw back. She was beautiful, but he ought to have had his fill of beautiful women after Conchita. Something about Maria's forthright, open manner appealed to him. But he had never questioned Conchita's honesty either, until he had broken José out of San Quentin and returned to their house. Then it had been too late to do anything about her lying ways.

"You want to ask me something," Slocum said. "Murrieta did, too, but he never got around to it."

"Why do you say that?"

"You don't live here—"

"No!"

"And you just happened to bring news of two men fighting that Murrieta had to referee. I think there was more to it. You wanted to come to find out if he had asked me something."

"Everything Procipio has said about you is true," she said. "He said you were very smart." She looked down at his Colt. "And that you were a gunfighter."

"Not much of either these days," Slocum said. "You're not wanting to hire me as a gunman, are you? I don't sell my gun."

"No, no," she said, shaking her head and causing a halo of raven's wing dark hair to float about her head. "You went into San Quentin to rescue another, no?"

"That's true," Slocum said, wishing it wasn't. "I'm not doing that again."

"But there is one inside who does not deserve to be there."

"Your lover?"

"I have not had a lover in many months."

"Brother?"

"*Un primo*, a cousin."

"He's in jail?"

"Where Procipio was. Where you were. San Quentin."

Slocum said nothing as he studied the lines of her face. She had high cheekbones and lips meant to be kissed. He had done that before, and it had landed him in a world of trouble. But Maria was so innocent looking.

"Innocent."

This unsettled him. It was as if she had read his mind.

"That was what I—"

"Please, you must help Procipio—and me." Maria moved closer and reached out. Her small hand rested on his. He started to pull away, but she gripped down with surprising strength.

Slocum had been in the same position before, but Conchita had made her plea after she had ensnared him with her wiles. Maria made her desires known up front.

"You are a very powerful man," she said softly. "I am drawn to men such as you."

"Killers?"

"Lady killers," she said, smiling. What might have been a wicked smile carried that shyness and a hint of anticipation to it that Slocum found irresistible. A thousand thoughts raced through his mind, and he saw from Maria's reaction that many of those raced through hers, too.

He kissed her.

He kissed her and damned himself for being a fool. Thinking with his *cojones*, Murrieta had said, and it was true and Slocum didn't care.

They both stood, still awkwardly kissing. Then they flowed into each other's arms, her soft, yielding body pressed hotly against his. If Murrieta had wanted Maria to convince him to do whatever it was, he wouldn't return— or he might to "surprise" them and blackmail Slocum into joining what would be a crazy plot.

If Murrieta knew nothing and returned, he might consider this embrace to be worth killing Slocum over. The man obviously took his duty as *alcalde* seriously, and protecting the citizens, especially the lovely young señoritas, would be a priority.

All this crossed Slocum's mind, and he didn't care. Maria's lips tasted like honey against his. Her fingers began exploring, moving up and down his back, pressing into his spine, then working higher to cradle the back of his head.

His own kiss deepened, and his tongue invaded her mouth. Their tongues dueled erotically, causing them both to breathe faster. He felt her heart trip-hammering through her breast crushed against his chest. He pulled her even closer, as if their bodies could merge this way. But they couldn't. Not like this.

He reached down and caught at her skirt, lifting it high. For her part, Maria worked frantically on his fly. He stroked over her bare legs, moved up, and found the curves of her taut ass. When he realized she was having difficulty with his fly, he squeezed down on her rump, then abandoned her flesh to shuck off his gun belt and then pop open his fly. Barely had he sprung out, erect and ready, when her groping fingers circled him and tugged him in obvious need toward the spot still hidden by the roll of her skirt.

She lifted a leg and hooked it around his waist. This positioned them properly for him to slip back and forth and then find the lust-slickened slit that opened to accommodate him fully. As he entered her, a tremor passed through her from head to toe. She shivered deliciously and clung even more fiercely to him. With a tiny hop, she jumped up so both legs circled his waist.

He held her and turned about, supporting both their weights. Leaning back caused him to sink balls deep into her, then bending forward, he pulled out enough for her to sob out, "No, in, I need you in me!"

Moving awkwardly at first and then finding the right rhythm, he moved in and out of her as she clung to him. But he wasn't able to thrust the way he wanted—the way she wanted, too.

Her moans grew louder until he spun about and sat her down on the table. This allowed her to give up her grip around his waist and hike both feet to the edge of the table. From here, Slocum pistoned forward, sinking fully. Then he withdrew. Slowly. Every inch of his retreat caused a new ripple of desire to pass through her. He felt the heat within his loins and the pressures mounting as he made love to this lovely woman. She leaned back, supporting herself on her elbows, as he continued to lever his hips forward furiously, then withdraw slowly. This motion soon caused her to cry out in carnal release.

Slocum continued for a minute longer and then knew

he was going to get off at any instant. His body took over and he moved erratically, driving forward and pulling out in a rhythm dictated more by his own arousal than a desire to pleasure her.

He shoved forward, gasped, and spilled his seed. All around his hidden length, she crushed down on him, milking him, squeezing the last possible thrill out of their love-making as she could.

He stepped back and looked at Maria. Her face was flushed, and she had a smile that could only be described as angelic.

"You are so good," she said in a shaky voice. "I knew it would be like this."

Before Slocum could answer, he heard Murrieta outside arguing with someone. He quickly buttoned up and turned as the *alcalde* came back into the small house.

Murrieta looked at him and Maria curiously but did not show any displeasure. From his distracted expression, he might still be settling some dispute all the way across the village. Slocum was glad for that because he found Maria's presence equally distracting.

She had spun about and landed on her feet on the opposite side of the table.

"They can never settle their own feuds," Murrieta said in disgust. "I do not know why I do this, this judging so others can lead peaceful lives. All it brings to me is trouble."

"But some trouble is worthwhile," Maria said. Her response might have been to Murrieta's woes, but Slocum knew she directed it to him.

"If it doesn't get you killed," Slocum said, "it might be worth it."

"It won't," Maria mouthed.

Slocum wasn't sure he believed her.

9

"The banker Galworthy is responsible for our woes," Procipio Murrieta said. "I care little that Valenzuela stole from the bank. He only beat me to it!"

"You ought to care, and not because the vault is empty. If the banker gets his dander up, he's likely to come after your property. You said you hadn't made the mortgage payments for a spell," Slocum pointed out.

"The crops are meager," Murrieta said, shrugging in resignation. "We do what we can but must have more water. We survive—barely. The times I am sent to prison do not help either. The entire village suffers."

Slocum looked from the man to Maria, who stood in the doorway. The afternoon sun lit her like an actress on a stage. Slocum listened to Murrieta with half an ear, his thoughts more on Maria and their brief time together. He thought he had learned his lesson with Conchita but now wasn't so sure. Maria was different—except she wanted something from him, too. She had mentioned the man in San Quentin put there by the banker, who now would be coming after others in this sleepy town with no name.

Slocum had a horse, he had his freedom, and if he had half a brain, he would leave when Murrieta and the others went to sleep that night. From everything he had seen, the village was less a farming community than an armed camp. Somehow he had left the company of bank robbers and thieves and now found himself amid rebels with Murrieta the leader of a peasant revolt. This wasn't his fight, no matter what payment Maria so willingly offered.

Still, he couldn't take his eyes off her. She was gorgeous.

". . . put into prison as a warning for us. Do not fight, that is the message."

"Prison?" Slocum's attention snapped back to what the *alcalde* was saying.

"Atencio is scheduled to be hanged. The banker railroaded him. Atencio is no more guilty than any of us, but Galworthy chose him as an example."

"Galworthy's the banker," Slocum said, piecing together the snippets he remembered hearing. He had to leave before he got himself involved to the point where he could never dig out. "What is Atencio supposed to have done?"

"Horse stealing, robbery, many other things I do not understand."

"He had a trial?"

Murrieta threw up his hands, then slammed them palms down on the table.

"If you call it a trial. The judge refused to let Atencio's lawyer say a word."

"So he had a lawyer? How'd you pay for him?"

"He took the case for nothing. *Por nada.* And that is what came of it."

"Never heard of a lawyer doing such a thing," Slocum said. His experience with lawyers showed them to be greedy bastards. Maybe this one was so inept he would take any case.

"He has political ambitions. He said so. He comes here to tell us how he fought for Atencio, how we need to change the laws and he is the one to do so if we vote for him."

Slocum wondered if the lawyer had tried very hard to free his client. Not only wasn't there money on the table, but a loss set him up to garner votes from Murrieta's village to remedy the outrage.

"What do you want of me?" Slocum asked. He was tired of hearing all the details. He wanted to know what Murrieta had in mind. Twice the *alcalde* had saved him, and he felt he owed the man something. Just how much would depend on what Murrieta asked.

"Atencio is to be hanged," Murrieta said. "I want help in breaking him out before this happens. If we can get him here, we can be sure he returns to Mexico, where he would be safe."

Slocum looked out at Maria. She was anxious, shifting from one foot to the other and back.

"This Atencio is her cousin?"

Murrieta's eyebrows arched, and he looked over his shoulder at Maria.

"You have learned much while you have been in my village," Murrieta said, turning back. "Does this matter?"

"No, not at all," Slocum said. "I owe you my life, or if not my life, then my freedom. Twice you came to my aid when you didn't have to. But I'm not pretending to be a convict to get back inside those walls." Slocum closed his eyes and perfectly pictured the stone walls rising around the prison. It was imposing from the outside. Looking at those walls with the guard towers from inside suffocated hope and destroyed his soul. Better to die in a gunfight than to let them lock him up again.

"I understand this. The escape through the wall is something to be done only once."

"By now," Slocum said, "they probably have it completely sealed off. No doorway, completely concreted and stoned."

"You are a clever man, John Slocum. You can come up with another way to save Atencio. He is not to be hanged for another week."

Slocum inwardly groaned. A week was hardly time to come up with a rescue plan. They might need dynamite to blow open the gate or more firepower than all the *peones* in this village could provide, even if Murrieta risked his entire peasant army. San Quentin was a fortress designed not only to keep prisoners inside but to keep out those wanting to rescue them.

"Would there be any chance your lawyer could get a stay of execution?"

"Pah," Murrieta said, waving his hand about in dismissal. "He would not bother."

Slocum frowned in concentration then said, "What if the banker told the judge he made it all up?"

"Why should he? He wants our land. It is nothing to him if Atencio dies in prison, disgraced."

"A man who desires money that much can be bought."

"We cannot pay our mortgages. How can we bribe him?"

"The Valenzuelas robbed his bank," Slocum said, thinking aloud. "They have money he'd want back."

"So you would rob them?"

Slocum smiled. That thought had crossed his mind more than once. They owed him for the time he had spent in San Quentin, and the entire loot taken from Galworthy's bank would be a good start. He wanted more from them— and Conchita—but taking what they had stolen would be a beginning. If the money could free Atencio, it would relieve Slocum of a debt to Murrieta even if it wouldn't give him a pair of coins to rub together for his trouble.

"That might work, unless they have hightailed it out of town," Slocum said. Somehow he thought Conchita would remain in the area. And why not? Sheriff Bernard thought he had robbed the bank because of her lying testimony. The Valenzuela family was free to do as they pleased, and somehow Slocum doubted they were finished yet even if José was sought as an escaped prisoner from San Quentin.

Before he could say another word, Maria hissed and caught Murrieta's attention. The man leaped to his feet, grabbed a rifle, and told Slocum, "Do not come out. We will take care of this."

Slocum got to his feet and cautiously peered out. Into what served as a town square—the community water well was there—rode Sheriff Bernard and four deputies. All the men carried rifles or shotguns resting in the crooks of their left arms. They were ready for a fight. Slocum considered giving it to them. Getting rid of the tenacious sheriff might not solve all his problems, but it would cause enough confusion in Miramar and throughout the county that he could get the hell away.

"We're looking for an escaped prisoner," Bernard called.

"We are poor farmers," Murrieta said, not a hint of guilt in his voice. Slocum marveled at this since Murrieta might well fit the description of the lawman's quarry.

"I know all about that," Bernard said. "Hez Galworthy tells me all the time I got to serve process on you people."

"You are here, then, to steal our land?"

"I told you that I'm looking for a prisoner that escaped from my jail. I don't rightly care about other escapees." Bernard made it obvious he hadn't come for Murrieta, though he had to know the man had escaped from San Quentin.

Slocum melted back into the small house, looked around for a way out, and realized there was only one door. The few windows were high and small, hardly wide enough for him to squeeze through. If the sheriff figured out he was inside, he was a goner.

He drew his six-shooter and waited.

"You know everyone here, Sheriff," Murrieta said.

"Now, that's not true. I don't know you, and here you're acting as mouthpiece for everyone."

"Maybe I am your escaped prisoner?"

Bernard cleared his throat, then winked broadly.

"Nope, never saw you in my town. The gent I'm looking for is named Jasper Jarvis, though I wonder about how true that is. Turn him over to me and I still won't know any of you next time I ride this way." Bernard looked hard at Murrieta to make sure he understood the meaning. Cooperating with Wilkinson and the warden at San Quentin wasn't on his plate, then or ever, but capturing a man who had escaped from his jail was, especially if he was suspected of robbing the Miramar bank.

"Why do you come here?" Murrieta swung his rifle around to emphasize his point. He wanted the posse gone from his village. Slocum wished he would start shooting. Blood would be spilled but all the lawmen would be permanently removed from the hunt for him.

"We got a note to the effect that he's holed up in your town. Said Jarvis was responsible for a whole slew of crimes. Robbed Hez Galworthy's bank, maybe beat up a prison guard. Fact is, Jarvis is wanted by more people than you can shake a stick at. But he's mine first. Them varmints up at San Quentin can wait their turn."

"He is not here."

"Got to look."

"You cannot do this without a search warrant!"

"Now aren't we the dirt farmer lawyer? This note says he's hiding out here, so I'm searching the entire village before he can get away." Bernard studied Murrieta long and hard and finally said, "Might be I'm beginning to recognize you."

Murrieta walked to the sheriff and took the note. He crumpled it up and tossed it to the ground.

"That is not a legal paper."

"As legal as I need, Murrieta. You want to start shooting? You'll never win."

Slocum saw the deputies already on the ground and moving to other houses. The sheriff eyed where Slocum hid in a way that betrayed the first house to be searched. Slocum looked for a trapdoor, hoping for a root cellar. Nothing but dirt rewarded his search. Even a prairie dog couldn't dig a tunnel out of there fast enough. Murrieta might shoot the sheriff in the back if he came in, but Slocum wanted to avoid that. Drawing attention to the town would bring federal marshals down on them. Murrieta was sure to be sent back to San Quentin if the investigation went far enough.

He stood on the table and rammed his fingers into the thatch of the roof. Working furiously, he opened a hole to the roof, then jumped, caught a viga, and pulled himself up and onto the flat roof. From his vantage he saw Bernard dismount and come to the door. A small scuffle ensued between the lawman and Murrieta, then Maria tried to stop Bernard. That ended the same way the one with Murrieta had.

Sheriff Bernard stepped into the small house, rifle ready to fire on Jasper Jarvis.

Slocum worked back the thatch as fast as he could. A small hole still remained, allowing him to stare down at the top of the sheriff's hat. Slocum stretched to block as much of the sunlight as he could so it wouldn't call attention to the gaping roof. He held his breath as Bernard rummaged about, doing everything that Slocum had looking for a hiding spot.

Maria came in and demanded, "Go! You have no right!"

Slocum saw his boot prints in the center of the table. If the sheriff saw them, he would know in a flash where his escaped prisoner had gone.

"I want that son of a bitch back in the lockup. Excuse my language, ma'am."

Maria moved and perched on the edge of the table to keep Bernard from seeing the betraying footprints.

"You must do your duty. But you will not find this man in our village," she said hotly. "We are honest people."

Bernard pursed his lips and nodded, turned, and left. He joined his posse searching the other houses. When he was finished, he mounted. Slocum had to press himself flat since the low roof was almost at the sheriff's eye level.

"If you see any suspicious strangers, you let me know, you hear?"

"The only suspicious ones are in front of me now," Murrieta said.

"Don't get too cocky. Might just be Sergeant Wilkinson can find himself an escapee or two if *he* pokes around here."

With that threat, Bernard led his posse from the town. Slocum waited until the sun sank lower and he wouldn't be so obvious, then went to the edge of the roof and jumped to the ground. He landed hard and stayed in a crouch. At the far side of the bean field he caught sight of someone astride a horse, watching.

"It is nothing," Murrieta said. "I do not know who that is. Some woman. Not one of the posse."

As Slocum stood, the rider vanished. For a brief moment, she was caught in the dying sunlight. Conchita Valenzuela.

He picked up the crumpled sheet Murrieta had discarded, unwrinkled it the best he could, and read the carefully written words. He had seen such handwriting before. It was Conchita's.

"If we're going to free Atencio, we have to do it fast," Slocum said. The longer he remained in this village, the more time Conchita and José had to think of ways to bring the law down on his head. Eventually Wilkinson or others from San Quentin would arrive. When that happened, Murrieta would be at risk, too.

Slocum looked down the road where Bernard had ridden off and shook his head. Bernard knew Murrieta was an escaped prisoner from San Quentin. But he cared only for the one man who had gotten away from his own jail in Miramar. How long this disregard for other lawmen could go on, Slocum didn't know.

"We have to get Atencio out real fast."

10

"He will rob us. He is that kind of man," Procipio Murrieta said in disgust.

Slocum had no other plan.

"If the banker doesn't drop the charges and fess up how he lied, Atencio doesn't have much of a chance," Slocum pointed out. "We ransom him. The banker is greedy, if you've read him a'right."

"I have. Nothing makes his eyes glow more than the sight of gold. Bars, coins, he does not care. Even worthless paper money makes him pant like a rabid dog."

Slocum had to laugh at that. It could have been the description of any banker. He sobered as he considered how he had to get the money stolen from the Miramar bank. He had to rob José, Conchita, and their father. For all he knew, they had spent the money quickly rather than hiding it, but somehow he didn't think Conchita was the kind to let her brother or any other man squander a stack of coins.

"We might have to use the lawyer as a go-between.

The banker is mighty intent on seeing me arrested for the theft, and he might think I'd had a change of heart."

"It does not seem fair, stealing this money and then giving it back to a man like Galworthy," Murrieta said. "But if it is the only way to free Atencio before his execution, then this is what we must do."

Slocum understood the situation fully. Giving up money, if he recovered it from the Valenzuelas, rankled him as much as it did Murrieta. Maybe for a different reason. He would keep it for his trouble, for all Conchita and her family had put him through. The time in San Quentin had to be paid for somehow. But Murrieta undoubtedly thought it was a shame returning money to a man he loathed. Galworthy would foreclose on their farms in a heartbeat and cared little for how he got the stolen money back.

"What's your lawyer's name? I'd like to avoid using him if we can, but someone who's on the right side of the law might come in handy as our negotiator."

"Michael Durant," Murrieta said as if the name burned his tongue. "I do not know what more he could have done to keep Atencio from the gallows, but there must have been something. A law, a loophole as they say. Durant did not try hard enough."

"You just saying that or are you sure? He might have been paid off by the banker," Slocum said.

"That is possible. I do not understand much of what was said in the court. It is only a way to imprison us, not help us."

"Or stick your necks into a noose," Slocum said, nodding. He got the same feeling about most courts and judges. Lawyers argued tiny points and let the big ones fall by the wayside in their attempts to look smarter than their opposition.

"How do you find the Valenzuelas, much less the loot from the bank?" Murrieta asked.

"I doubt they returned to the house where I took José,"

Slocum said. He looked up to see Maria frown. She started to speak, then clamped her lips tightly.

"What have you heard?" Slocum demanded.

"Nothing of them," the woman said, "but there is another thing that I overheard in town."

"In Miramar?" Slocum asked. She nodded and then rushed to tell what she had learned.

"There is a stagecoach coming with a great deal of money in it. It is for the Army in the Presidio."

"Why isn't it being brought in by ship?" Slocum asked.

"There was a fire aboard a ship to the south. It sank quickly. Perhaps it had the garrison payroll on it," Murrieta said. "I heard this but did not know of any money being brought by land." He looked hard at Maria. "Where did you hear this?"

"I was leaving the office of Durant. I had gone to plead with him to help Atencio."

"What did you . . . pay?" Murrieta half stood and leaned forward, fists on the table. Slocum rocked back, surprised at the man's vehemence.

"Nothing, Procipio, nothing! I swear! The men I overheard were talking of a telegram. The telegrapher himself was taking the message to the bank."

"That's the kind of bait I need to lure the Valenzuelas from hiding," Slocum said. "When's the stage due to pass through?"

"Any time now," Maria said. "The schedule is for one this very afternoon, but it might be that the money is with another."

"They wouldn't send along a cavalry detachment to protect it," Slocum said, his mind racing to figure all the angles, to find all the pitfalls. "Every gang in California would go after it then. It's being shipped from Los Angeles?" He saw the quick glance between Procipio and Maria, then the woman fixed her deep, dark ebony eyes on him.

"I do not know. Where is all the Army money kept?"

"Doesn't matter," Slocum said. "Here's my plan." He began building on a sketchy idea. Procipio was as skeptical as Maria was hopeful that his wild-ass scheme would work.

"You ought to be a highwayman," Slocum said. "This is the perfect spot for a robbery."

"That was my father," Procipio said indignantly. "I farm and that is all I want from life."

"Didn't mean anything by it," Slocum said, his attention fixed on the way the road made a hairpin turn and the boulders on either side. Those rocks could protect the stage and driver but also provided an excellent spot for a rifleman to take out any guard who refused to surrender. One robber need only stand in the road to stop the progress up the trail while an accomplice did the necessary work if the driver or shotgun messenger protested. The tight notch in the road prevented the driver from wheeling the stage about and trying to run, as if any driver would. Being held up on a California route was an all-too-often occurrence. If the driver surrendered his cargo, the highwaymen obliged by not killing him and his passengers.

"I was falsely put into San Quentin," Murrieta went on. "Just as Atencio was, though they did not see fit to frame me for horse thieving."

"Hush," Slocum said, motioning Murrieta back. Two riders trotted into the notch from the direction of Miramar. They were ten miles outside town, about perfect for a stagecoach robbery. The more Slocum saw of this location, the more envious he became of whoever could launch a robbery here. It was as close to perfect as he had ever seen for thievery.

The two riders stopped and looked around. Both had bandannas pulled up over their faces, but this was to protect them from the blowing dust rather than hide their identities. They exchanged words too low for Slocum to hear, then split up. One rode back down the road and stepped down from his horse. He took out a rifle, cocked it, then went to the middle of the road.

The second rider wended his way up into the rocks to the very spot Slocum had picked out as ideal for an ambush.

"That's José," Slocum said softly. Murrieta nodded, then reached for his six-shooter. Slocum grabbed the man's brawny wrist and forced him to leave his gun in its holster. "We wait."

Murrieta grumbled but relaxed, sliding back to a spot where José Valenzuela could not see him if the *bandido* chose to look around.

"How will we capture them?" Murrieta asked. "I should go to the road and—"

"We're not going to catch them. After they rob the stage, they'll take the loot back to their hideout. Their new hideout," Slocum explained.

"Where they might have the gold from the bank?"

"Exactly," Slocum said. He was all keyed up, as if he were the one doing the robbery. How much would the payroll be for an entire Army garrison? He couldn't tell. There might be enough for both Fort Point and the Presidio. The stagecoach shipment might be thousands of dollars. After he followed the Valenzuelas back to their lair, he would have to consider letting Murrieta use the gold to free Atencio and keeping this haul for himself.

A pang of conscience poked him. He might give some to Murrieta for his village. Maria might decide to ride out with him as he worked his way north away from San Quentin and the nastiness he had found there. The two of them could spend the money in delightful ways. The more Slocum chewed on this prospect, the more he liked it.

He felt a distant vibration echo through to hard rock under his palm. Pressing his ear to the rock, he strained to discern a pattern. A slow smile came to his lips. The rumble of stage wheels was unmistakable. In less than ten minutes the Valenzuelas would put their plan into effect.

Then he would see how well honed his tracking skills were following them. Chances were good they had a route chosen over rocky terrain to throw off trackers in a posse, but traces would remain for a short time. They counted on the sheriff taking hours or even a day to get his deputies on their trail. Slocum wouldn't let the spoor blow away. He was good enough to track a snowflake through a blizzard; the Valenzuelas weren't anywhere near as respectable at hiding their trail as he was at finding it.

"They attack!" Murrieta rose and stared at the pair of highwaymen. Slocum saw the expression on Murrieta's face and saw something close to longing. He wanted to be down there sticking up the stage as much as Slocum did.

Gunfire rolled through the narrow gap and echoed up to the two watching the drama unfold. Slocum touched the ebony handle of his six-shooter but did not draw. Those bullets were not aimed at him. José Valenzuela fired methodically until the driver reined in his team. The horses kicked up a cloud of dust that took a while to settle.

When it did, Slocum saw the driver sagged down in the box, holding his belly. The passengers shoved six-shooters out and fired, but the angle was wrong. José took them out one by one until they finally surrendered.

"Throw out your guns!" José cried. He waved to his pa, who advanced, rifle leveled. "Give him all your money!"

"He steals everything from the passengers. The payroll is not enough!" Murrieta seemed outraged. "How dare they take from poor travelers?"

Slocum found himself agreeing, but for a different reason. The payroll had to be the most valuable thing aboard that stage. Seizing it and getting the hell away counted for more than the few dollars the Valenzuelas would get off the passengers. The gunfire might draw others to see what was happening. The sheriff might even be in the area with his posse.

He turned grim at that thought. Sheriff Bernard still hunted for the man he thought had robbed the Miramar bank: John Slocum.

"Die!" screeched José Valenzuela. He opened fire on the tight knot of passengers, cutting them down where they stood with hands held high over their heads. "Get the strongbox!"

"It is secured with chains," his father called. "I must shoot it off."

"Shoot the wood, not the chains. You do not want to be hit by a ricochet."

José slid down the rock and landed hard in front of the stage. The driver moaned and tried to lift his head. The elder Valenzuela shot him three times. The driver slumped down into the box. Slocum didn't need to check for a pulse. José Valenzuela's pa had just murdered an injured man, as his son had shot down the helpless passengers.

José vanished and several rifle shots echoed out. Then came a grunt and both men dragged a heavy iron box with chains tangled around it into sight. Slocum tensed, reaching for his Colt, but he relaxed and let the pair continue to haul away their ill-gotten gains.

"They murdered those who had already surrendered," Murrieta said in horror. "That is an unspeakable crime!"

"Nobody said they were pure as the wind-driven snow," Slocum said. "Come on." He skidded down a steep, rocky incline to where they had left their horses. Turning to Murrieta, he said, "You get on back to your village. This is my chore now. I'll get you when I find where they're hiding."

"Where they hide the gold," Murrieta corrected.

Slocum swung into the saddle. Murrieta looked up at him and said, "Take care, amigo. If not for your own sake, then for Maria's. She has become very fond of you."

With that, Murrieta mounted and rode off without so much as a backward look. Slocum settled his hat, thinking hard on what the man had said. Then he grinned. It was good that Maria thought of him what he did of her. With a quick tug on the reins, he got his horse started along a narrow trail that wended about before coming down to the main road a quarter mile from where the holdup had occurred.

Slocum looked back and saw the stagecoach team snorting and pawing nervously at the ground. They didn't understand all the gunfire or why their driver wasn't urging them forward. From the way the carrion birds were already spiraling downward, the driver and passengers wouldn't be going anywhere but into buzzards' gizzards.

Looking away from the stage, he turned his attention to the road. Finding the Valenzuelas' trail was simple. They had galloped off. Since he didn't see any trace of the box, he knew they had taken it with them. That would slow their escape. Slocum trotted off, being careful not to overtake them. A smile came to his lips when he lost their trail on the road. He backtracked and saw that they had doubled back before leaving the road. He used his spurs to get his horse down into a ditch and then up the far side. The Valenzuelas had jumped the ditch rather than taking the slow way Slocum had. But he found the deep hoofprints where the horses had landed and galloped away.

He trotted along, eyes on the tracks leading uphill and into a wooded area. Slocum drew rein and studied the edge of the copse to be sure he didn't ride into an ambush. The two road agents had shown they had no hesitation killing wantonly. He finally rode ahead, fairly certain they hadn't slowed in their escape to lay a trap for anybody who might be on their trail. Since he hadn't seen anyone, he knew the Valenzuelas hadn't either.

Tracking them in the wooded area would be more difficult since the pine needles carpeting the ground didn't take hoofprints well. Slocum knew a few tricks to keep him close behind the fleeing father and son.

He wove in and out of the sparsely spaced trees, then stopped when he heard voices ahead. This surprised him since he had expected the two men to ride for some time into the hills. Having a hideout this close to the road seemed wrong.

Then he recognized one voice and went cold inside.

"You sure he's headed this way?" Sheriff Bernard asked.

"I saw him," Conchita Valenzuela said. "He is a dangerous man. You are sure you will be safe, Sheriff?"

"Got a couple boys riding with me," Bernard said. "A gunshot and they'll come running."

"You would not want that shot to be through your heart. He is a robber and a killer. You can see it in his eyes."

"Might be you can. I gotta go with what I read about him. This here Jasper Jarvis doesn't look to be all that dangerous."

They continued arguing over how dangerous he— Jarvis—was as Slocum veered away through the woods. Tracking the fleeing outlaws meant less to him right now than avoiding the law. He had no reason to shoot it out with the sheriff or his posse but would if it came to that. He wasn't going to stand trial for a bank robbery he didn't commit, and he sure as hell wasn't going back to San Quentin.

He began curving in a wide arc to take him back toward the road but slowed when he heard horses behind him. Several horses. He didn't think the sheriff was behind him but the rest of the posse still rattled around nearby.

"There he is! I see the varmint!"

Slocum put his head down and raked his horse's flanks with his heels to rocket forward. Tree limbs slashed at him, and bloody scratches exploded on his arms, face, and body as he rode hard for daylight.

From their hoots and hollers, Slocum knew the riders were closing the gap and bearing down on him. He rode faster, cursing his bad luck—and that lying bitch Conchita Valenzuela.

11

"There he is, boys. Git 'im!"

Another branch lashed Slocum across the face, almost knocking him from his horse. He half turned and chanced a quick look behind. He saw the dun and paint coats of two horses flashing through the trees. He hugged his own horse's neck and guided it at an angle away from the line where he had been riding so frantically. Gradually slowing his breakneck pace allowed him to hear the deputies in the woods complaining about having lost his trail. Slocum finally brought his horse to a halt. Its sides heaved as lather formed.

He had pushed the horse to its limit then realized how close he was to his own. Sweat drenched his shirt and vest. His coat clung fiercely to his body, glued in place by both sweat and blood. With deliberate slowness, he turned his horse along his back trail and waited to see if the posse would find him.

Their sounds faded away. They had kept riding toward the road—his original destination until he had realized how difficult it would have been to outrun them. Once he had burst from the trees, he would have been exposed for almost a quarter mile. Even the feckless deputies could have spotted him.

Once his horse had rested, he gingerly guided it back into the woods, cutting through on a path that should have taken him across the Valenzuelas' tracks. He had gold to find. And maybe two outlaws to kill. Slocum had ridden less than a half mile when he heard voices again.

". . . my men went tearing off like hounds after a rabbit. Since they haven't returned, I'd better go find them," Sheriff Bernard said.

"They are lost?" Conchita spoke with a mixture of caring undercut with derision. Slocum didn't have to see her lovely face to know her lip was upturned in a sneer. She thought little of the deputies' ability. For all that, Slocum wasn't too impressed either. They had almost caught him, but it had been his own damn-fool eagerness to find José and his father that'd been responsible. Nothing the deputies had done counted as cleverness or skill on their part.

But Slocum had a modicum of respect for Sheriff Bernard. The man was astute enough to know he had to keep after Slocum, even if he thought his name was Jasper Jarvis. More than this, Slocum admired the way Bernard had stood up to Sergeant Wilkinson. The prison guard was a formidable opponent and an imposing figure. Bernard hadn't batted an eye telling him when he caught Jarvis he'd stand trial for bank robbery. Only then could San Quentin claim his suspect.

Slocum came to the edge of a clearing. Not fifty feet away Conchita and Bernard sat astride their horses, looking away in the direction of the road. Trees blocked a direct view, but Bernard had figured out the direction his men had taken.

"You will catch him, Sheriff? This awful man Jarvis?"

"'Less he hightails it out of the county, I'll nab him. I promise you that, Miss Valenzuela."

"You have posted a reward? Or has the banker man?"

"Galworthy wants him bad, but he wants his gold back even more. Galworthy put a fifty-dollar reward out on Jarvis and a thousand-dollar reward for the return of everything stolen from his bank." Bernard laughed heartily. "Now what sort of idiot would return five thousand dollars in gold coins for a thousand-dollar reward in scrip?"

"An honest man?" suggested Conchita.

Slocum almost shouted out, "Where'll you find one of them in this state?" However, he held his tongue and waited for the two riders to drift toward the far side of the clearing. When they entered the woods, he heaved a sigh of relief. The posse was too prideful to admit they had lost him. Instead, they'd either lie about charging after anyone or claim it was only a deer they chased. Either way, they weren't likely to return.

He wasn't as certain about the sheriff and knew that Conchita had to join her family eventually. Riding about in a circle failed to reveal any tracks. He ruefully admitted he had lost José and his father. That put his plan into a cocked hat, unless he got lucky. That didn't seem too likely since he had just used up what luck he had avoiding the posse and the sheriff.

"Conchita," he said softly. She was his ticket to the hideout and the loot from both the stagecoach robbery and Galworthy's bank.

Slocum looked around, found a spot where he could watch the clearing when the woman returned and get some idea which direction she chose to follow her brother and pa. He rode to the thicket, dismounted, and took time to drink some water from his canteen and even sit down to rest. He was bleeding from dozens of scratches from his romp through the forest, and the last branch had whacked him hard enough to give him a headache now that the excitement was over and done.

Leaning back against a tree trunk, he closed his eyes to rest them for a moment. When he snapped alert, he reached for his six-shooter, thinking something was seriously wrong. Panic died down when he realized the hit on the head hadn't left him blind. His eyes were wide open, but it was to a forest veiled in night. He had passed out for most of the day, missing Conchita's return. Worse, he had been a sitting duck if the sheriff's men had come back.

Or José Valenzuela. The man had gunned down the stagecoach passengers without provocation. There was no telling how deep his vicious streak ran. Finding Slocum passed out would be a godsend for him.

If Conchita had found him, she would have summoned the sheriff to take him off to the lockup again. She was far cleverer than her brother and knew Slocum being in jail got them off the hook. Bernard would stop looking for bank robbers if he thought he had one behind bars.

Body aching from being in one position all afternoon long, he climbed to his feet and led his rested horse out into the clearing. If the sheriff and Conchita had been there talking, José and their pa would have ridden through the woods some distance away. Conchita would have distracted the lawman until they had reached a trail to take them to their hideout.

Slocum spent the rest of the night searching for that trail and couldn't find it. He reluctantly came to admit the Valenzuelas had outsmarted him—and they hadn't even known they were doing it.

Or was it Conchita who had gotten the better of him? He had her pegged as being the brains in that family.

Finally mounting, he rode slowly to the road. By now the robbery would be known all the way to Miramar. Slocum rode to the rocky notch in the road and saw inky spots in the dust where the passengers had bled. The starlight didn't give him much illumination, but he didn't need it. He had seen what happened earlier. Not sure what he was looking for, he rode back and forth a dozen times before giving up.

Only then did he turn toward Murrieta's village. Telling him of his failure didn't set well with Slocum, but they had to come up with another scheme to keep Atencio from hanging. All the way back to the village Slocum thought hard on this and finally came up with another plan even more far-fetched than letting the Valenzuelas rob the stage and then track them to their hideout so he could rob them.

This time Slocum recognized his plan for what it was: pure desperation.

"I stole it from the clotheslines," Maria said, holding out the uniform and estimating how it would fit Slocum.

He eyed the prison guard's blue wool jacket with distaste. The brass buttons needed polishing, and the trousers with the jacket were far too short for his six-foot frame. Maria stepped closer, and he felt the heat from her body as she pressed against him, sizing up the waist. The trousers would go around his middle once and then half again over.

"I can sew in pleats," she said.

"Cut the cloth out and sew it onto the cuffs." Slocum looked down, and the bottom of the trousers were only a little more than midcalf. "I'll stick out like a sore thumb if you don't."

"I can do this," Maria said thoughtfully. She looked up at him, her face open and concerned. "Do you want to do such a brave thing for Atencio?"

He kissed her quickly, but she wouldn't have any of that tiny peck. She gave him a real kiss, hot and passionate, tongue working feverishly, lips crushing fiercely. Only when they heard Murrieta approaching, singing a song in his deep voice, did they part reluctantly.

"So," Murrieta said, seeing them inside the hut, "you have finally gotten into his pants?" Murrieta laughed. Slocum held back a surge of anger at him as Maria blushed furiously. She held out the pants and pointed silently to the jacket.

"If Atencio is due to be hanged at sundown, I've got to hurry," Slocum said. "Is everything ready?"

Murrieta looked stricken as he said, "I have done what I can. You are our savior, John Slocum."

"Only if I get him out." Slocum looked at his Colt Navy in its holster on the rickety table. He had to leave that behind. Guards inside San Quentin didn't carry firearms other than rifles. They relied on their truncheons, but Slocum didn't want to be burdened with one. Murrieta had given him three knives, which he was going to hide in case he needed them. Realistically, Slocum knew that if he was found out, three knives wouldn't be enough. A Gatling gun might not be enough to get away.

Not for the first time he cursed himself for agreeing to free Atencio. Then he looked at Murrieta and saw his desolation. Maria was even more wracked with anguish, making him reach out and touch her cheek. She pressed his fingers into her flesh, turned slightly, and kissed his hand.

"You will come back," she said in a choked voice.

"Fix the trousers," he said. She swallowed and then hurried away to cut out the extra material from the waist and tack it onto the cuffs so he wouldn't be noticed as easily.

He shrugged into the jacket. The sleeves were too short but were less noticeable if he left the front unbuttoned.

"You have sheaths for the knives," Murrieta said. "What else? A small pistol? You can hide it in the waistband."

Slocum remembered how floppy the waist would have been and said, "I could hide a couple rifles in there." He laughed. "I'll need a couple horses."

"I will get them. When you get Atencio out, you will need a spare."

"Make that four horses," Slocum said. Seeing Murrieta's surprise, he explained, "We will switch off when one gets tired. I said *we*, since you're coming with me. I need someone outside." He saw that Murrieta was shocked at the idea he had to do something to aid his friend.

"Atencio will need a spare," Murrieta said. "Will we need more? Each of us will ride with a spare to the prison, but leaving, we will have only one spare."

Slocum hoped it worked out that way. He strapped the knives into place, one on each leg and another along his left forearm. Then Maria returned with his pants. The pants fit better, but he would never pass close inspection. With luck, he wouldn't have to.

He ducked his head, went outside, and saw the four horses waiting for him. Procipio Murrieta was nothing if not a man of his word. Murrieta picked one of the horses and vaulted into the saddle. He wore crossed bandoliers with a six-shooter carried at either hip. Slocum hoped this firepower wasn't necessary, but better to have it and not need it than to find themselves lacking any way of shooting their way free.

Slocum mounted and headed north, with Murrieta riding as fast as he could to keep up. They had to reach San Quentin before Atencio got his neck stretched, and the ferry across the Golden Gate seldom ran on schedule.

"You cannot go to the front gate and ask to be let in. And it is almost sundown," Murrieta said, obviously worried.

"We've got an hour before he's to hang," Slocum said with more confidence than he felt. Murrieta was right. They had reached the front gate of the imposing prison but had no way of getting inside. Simply wearing the guard's uniform wasn't enough.

"Work gangs," Slocum said suddenly. "Are any sent outside the walls?"

"Not that I ever heard."

Slocum toyed with the idea of pretending to have captured Murrieta and immediately discarded it. Murrieta would be recognized immediately as an escaped prisoner, and Wilkinson would clap him in solitary too fast for Slocum to do anything. Worse, the sergeant might recognize Slocum, too.

"I hear a wagon," Slocum said, cocking his head to one side. On the late afternoon breeze came the faint rattling of chains and creaking wood of wheels bouncing along the rocky road. "Prisoner delivery?"

Murrieta shrugged eloquently.

"I'll find out. You stay out of sight. There. In that grove. I'll do what I can to get Atencio out, and you'd better be waiting with the horses. If you aren't, we're all going to hang."

Murrieta nodded and immediately rode away, leaving Slocum alone beside the road. The desolation he felt came from being trapped between the walls of a prison and oncoming guards. To return voluntarily to the far side of San Quentin's walls was the height of folly, yet Slocum was going to do just that. If he wanted to come out of this alive, he had to be bold and take the initiative.

He galloped away from the prison, hunting for the wagon. He found it just around a bend and barely out of sight of the prison guard towers.

The bed held four chained prisoners. The guard with a rifle perked up as Slocum rode toward the wagon. The rifle came up to the man's shoulder and Slocum waved frantically.

"Put that damned thing down. Don't shoot!"

"What do you want?" The guard was suspicious, but Slocum saw the one he had to convince was the driver, who glared hard at him.

He tried to remember if this was the same driver who'd delivered him to San Quentin what seemed a lifetime back. It might have been, but could the driver possibly remember every unwilling passenger? Slocum hoped not.

"You got a prisoner named José Valenzuela? Sergeant Wilkinson wants him double chained. He's a slippery one."

"Valenzuela? Naw, not this load." The guard glanced over his shoulder. Two prisoners were ginger-haired and possibly brothers. Another had the look of a sailor about him, and the fourth sat, knees drawn up and sobbing uncontrollably.

"What about that one?" Slocum said, pointing to the one crying.

"Name's Waring or Warren or something like that."

"What's wrong with him?" Slocum wanted to divert the guard's attention. It worked. He lowered his rifle so Slocum could breathe a tad easier.

"Don't cotton much to bein' convicted of murderin' the wife of a San Francisco politician. They was carryin' on and had a lovers' spat. Used a butcher knife on her, from what I hear."

"He killed her. He caught us, and he killed her and framed me!" the red-eyed prisoner cried out.

"They're all innocent," Slocum said.

"You get on back and tell Sergeant Wilkinson we ain't got his pet prisoner," the driver said.

"I'll just ride along. Not far to the front gates," Slocum said.

"Suit yourself." The driver mumbled under his breath, then said loud enough for Slocum to hear, "You guards always findin' new ways of malingerin'."

Slocum considered arguing for the sake of cementing his role as a guard but held back. The wagon rattled around the bend in the road and the sight of the walls took away his speech. He shook himself to clear his head. From here on, he had to be quick, respond properly, and get himself into the prison.

"Good to be back home," the armed guard said. "You want to go fetch the next batch of prisoners? Somethin' 'bout bein' outside the walls gives me the willies nowadays."

"We can talk about it," Slocum said. He was willing to go after more prisoners now.

"How many you got?" came the shout from high on the wall.

"Four."

"Open up," the guard called down. "We got more fish to swim in our pond!" He laughed at that, and the guard opening the gate was laughing, too.

Slocum forced himself to laugh, just to fit in.

"Let me help you," Slocum offered to the wagon guard.

"Much obliged, 'specially with *that* one." The guard pointed at the crying prisoner, who had once more descended into sobbing.

Slocum pulled the man out, got him on his feet, and moved so he kept the prisoners between him and the two guards coming from inside.

"Git 'em movin'. We ain't got all day."

Slocum shoved his prisoner ahead of him and passed through the gate, aware of other guards watching. Many of them tapped their truncheon against a thigh or slapped it against a palm in a drumbeat that chilled his blood.

"That way," Slocum said, steering the crying convict toward the processing area. He began to hang back and let the real guards do their duty.

Then he froze when a gruff voice called out, "You, the new guard. Come here!"

Slocum turned and saw Sergeant Wilkinson, his ledger tucked under his arm, pointing straight at him.

12

Slocum reached under the ill-fitting left coat sleeve and gripped the knife sheathed there. He would die but only after taking Wilkinson with him.

He stepped forward, but Wilkinson looked past him. Slocum veered away, his knife still hidden. Wilkinson bellowed again for the new guard to come to him.

Slocum let out pent-up breath when the guard with the rifle from the prison wagon marched forward.

"What you doin' violatin' regulations?" Wilkinson bellowed so loud that both guards and prisoners milling about in the yard some distance away all turned to see what caused the ruckus.

"Don't rightly know what you mean, Sergeant," the guard said.

"No firearms inside the prison, unless they are locked up where I can find and dispense them in a hurry," Wilkinson said. He continued to chew out the guard, giving Slocum a chance to drift even farther away until he was surrounded by other truncheon-tapping guards and a few sullen prisoners.

He made several quick turns intended to keep him out

of Wilkinson's line of sight, though he knew he attracted some attention because of his shoddy uniform. More than one prisoner looked at him and sniggered. Finally, a guard sauntered over and positioned himself so he blocked any further escape from Wilkinson's attention.

"Don't remember seein' you in here before," the guard said.

Slocum settled his uniform coat and moved his hand nearer the knife again. If he had to, he could gut the guard and toss away the knife so it would look as if a prisoner had killed him instead. The blood might be a problem, but Slocum doubted the other guards would be too observant if they thought they had the beginning of a prisoner riot on their hands.

"New," Slocum said.

"That's one crappy uniform you're wearin'. I wouldn't be caught dead in it." The guard laughed.

"Yours is pretty nice," Slocum allowed, "but I wouldn't want to be caught dead in it either." He half drew his knife when the guard stopped laughing. The flare of anger told of a killer no different from any of those locked up behind the prison walls.

"You got a mouth on you," the guard said. He slapped his truncheon against his thigh, as if testing how hard he could hit before bruising started.

"That the gallows where they're going to hang a prisoner?" Slocum pointed to the wood structure at the corner of the prison yard. The noose swung slowly in the faint late afternoon breeze, as if it had come alive and was searching for a neck to encircle.

"Now what else would we do with a gallows?" The guard glowered at him.

"What's his name? Atencio? The one getting his neck stretched today?"

"Don't know what they call him. Don't matter none to me."

"I used to be an executioner," Slocum said, an idea popping into his head. "Think anybody'd mind if I looked it over? For old times' sake?"

The guard's eyes went wide.

"You hung men? How many?"

Slocum sneered just a little as he said, "Not more 'n four. I got tired of riding a circuit, waiting for guilty verdicts. Then some towns did their own hanging. And vigilance committees? They always carry their own nooses, so that took away from my business. Thought it would pay better being a guard."

"Can. Depends on what you got to sell the cons. I—" The guard clamped his mouth shut when a whistle blew. "Damnation, exercise time's over already. Let's get them snakes back into their holes."

He went off to use his truncheon on the slower-moving prisoners, leaving Slocum alone in the yard. Taking advantage of the lull, Slocum walked to the gallows, trying not to draw unwanted attention. He kept his pace steady, not running and not moving too slow either. The gallows loomed high over him as he leaned against it. His heart hammered in his chest because he knew Atencio would be moved out here mighty soon and do a death jig unless something was done to save him.

Slocum had no idea how to do that. He was surrounded by guards willing to beat anyone to death that crossed them. If Sergeant Wilkinson spotted him, he would have the blue uniform ripped off and the prisoner's canvas with broad stripes substituted. He turned slowly to see any potential problems. He was alone.

Slipping around the side of the gallows, he ducked beneath the structure and looked up, hunting for some way to gimmick the trapdoor. As he stared up, slivers of blue California sky showing between the poorly fitted planks in the platform above, he knew this wouldn't accomplish anything. Any guard could come and fix the simple mechanism if he jammed it. Even nailing it shut wouldn't give him the result he wanted—Atencio's escape.

Getting the prisoner away from the gallows alive was only the first step in a long walk. They had to get outside San Quentin's walls to where Murrieta waited with the horses. And if Slocum couldn't get Atencio free, he had to escape himself. The task suddenly turned impossible.

He went up the thirteen steps to the platform and looked out on the empty yard. He doubted Warden Harriman would assemble the other prisoners to watch the execution. Only a handful of guards would join the warden as he sprung the trap and sent Atencio to the promised land.

Slocum caught the swaying noose and ran his callused fingers over it. The rough hemp was sturdy enough to support several men. It wasn't likely to break unless . . .

Slocum whipped out the knife sheathed along his forearm and began carefully picking away at the strands, leaving enough so that the rope appeared untouched while cutting much of the interior. Sweating from exertion, he finally released the rope and let it swing away like a pendulum. As it swung back, he saw two guards emerge from the main cell block, a shackled prisoner between them. Immediately behind came four others, including two guards and a well-dressed man Slocum took to be the warden. The fourth was a priest, working hard at his profession of saving a damned soul by muttering a constant prayer.

Not wasting any time, Slocum dropped down beside the gallows and waited. He worried that Wilkinson might be in the party, but the sergeant was nowhere to be seen. Counting slowly, gauging distances, Slocum waited until the proper moment to step out and fall in behind the guards immediately behind the warden. The two on either side of Atencio marched the condemned man to the platform.

The warden looked irritated as he took out his pocket watch and popped open the case to study the face. He clicked the lid shut and tucked the watch back into his vest pocket.

"Where is he?" The warden asked the question, but nobody answered. The two guards with him exchanged looks and kept quiet.

Slocum turned when he heard a commotion at the front gate. He caught his breath when he saw Wilkinson escorting a man in his Sunday best to the gallows.

"It's about time you got here, Mr. Durant," the warden said querulously.

"Are you in a hurry, sir? You have somewhere else to be? I assure you, my client is willing to let you attend to other business and postpone this until another day."

"Oh, shut up," the warden said. "You're here because you got the judge to let you witness the execution, nothing more." The warden spun and stalked up the steps.

Slocum turned to see him emerge on the side of the condemned. Atencio looked nervous but resolved to his fate. Slocum didn't turn away because that would bring him face to face with Sergeant Wilkinson. There might be an unscheduled execution if the guard recognized him.

"You've received the last rites of your faith. You have anything to say before I carry out your sentence for the state of California?"

Atencio shook his head. His knees buckled a little as the guards moved him onto the trapdoor. One fastened a sandbag around his ankles to make the drop hard and swift. The other placed the noose with the knot at one side, then added a black bag to hide his face.

The warden pushed one guard aside, gripped the lever with both hands, and yanked hard. Atencio fell like a stone. For a moment the rope remained taut, then it snapped where Slocum had cut through it. Beneath the platform Atencio cried out, gasping and choking and kicking.

"What the hell happened?" The warden shoved one guard to the steps. "Get him. Fetch the damned prisoner so we can do this again with another rope!"

"One moment!" Durant held up his hand as if he were

a schoolboy wanting his teacher's attention. "You can't hang him again. Not today. The law won't allow that!"

"The sentence was to hang him by the neck until he was dead."

"Once. You get one chance only," the lawyer said.

"Bullshit. He wasn't properly hanged, so we keep trying until he is. I don't care if it takes a hundred miles of rope!" The warden's face turned an ugly beet color as his ire rose.

"Double jeopardy," declared Durant. "You tried and failed. You can't execute him a second time."

"We didn't do a first time!" Froth flecked the warden's lips as he waved his arms around like a windmill.

"I'll see you a prisoner in this rat hole if you try to execute my client a second time."

The guards shifted uneasily as they held Atencio between them. The man's knees were bent, and he hobbled as they tried to walk him to the steps leading back to the platform. They hadn't bothered to remove the black hood.

"What are you saying, Durant?"

"I'll get a court order. There's no judge in this state who wouldn't agree that a new sentencing is necessary. You're not allowed to swing my client any number of times! Once! You get one try only!"

The priest edged closer to the warden and whispered to him. Slocum almost laughed when the furious warden cocked his fist back, as if to punch the padre. Then he dropped his arm to his side and came to the edge of the platform so he could glare down at the lawyer.

"Father Benjamin agrees with you. He said there's been something like this happen before."

"Precedence," Durant crowed.

"You get the hell out of my prison, you shyster."

"My client had better be in good condition when he's ordered back to court. If he's not, the judge will know the reason!"

"Get him out. Now, damn it, get him out of my prison!"

Slocum turned slowly so Wilkinson would already be facing toward the gate. For a heart-stopping instant they faced each other, but the sergeant's attention was on Atencio and the guards supporting him. He strode to them.

"This way," Slocum said, taking the lawyer's arm and pulling him toward the front gate.

Durant jerked free and shouted over his shoulder, "You're not to touch one hair on his head! I'm warning you."

This time he let Slocum herd him to the gate. The entire way the lawyer grumbled and cursed.

"You think you can get him out of here?" Slocum asked.

"What? Don't be an ass. He's guilty as sin. The best I can hope for is to gain a stay of execution and keep him alive for another week. I need to get better press out of this. The *Alta California* is making fun of me and destroying my reputation over this. Hanging a horse thief!" Durant smoothed out his coat and walked, chin high to the gate. He stopped there, waiting for Slocum to open it.

He worked to open the small door set in the larger one designed to let in wagons. When he swung it open, Durant ducked through. Slocum followed. For a moment, he couldn't believe it was going to be this easy. But it was. Slocum slipped through and pulled it to behind him.

"You can get an extra week before they try to hang him again?" Slocum asked.

Durant didn't bother to reply. He climbed into his buggy and rattled away. Slocum sidled along the wall, then headed toward the trees where Murrieta waited. He hadn't gotten Atencio free, but the man hadn't been hanged either. They had an extra week to figure out how to get him out of the prison.

Somehow the prospect looked even bleaker now than it had before.

13

"What is wrong? Where is he?" Procipio Murrieta grabbed Slocum by the front of the uniform and shook.

Slocum batted the man's hands away and considered taking a swing at him. He wasn't in a good mood, and having Murrieta act like this did nothing to smooth his ruffled feathers.

"He got a stay of execution. One week," Slocum said. He went on to explain all that had happened. The expression on Murrieta's face flowed like butter melting in the sun, going from elation to despair and finally matching Slocum's own.

"We cannot hope to be so lucky to get into the prison this way again," Murrieta said. "He will be executed." He heaved a deep sigh. "You did what you could. That is all anyone could ask."

"That lawyer fellow," Slocum said. "He didn't have to come to the prison yard for the hanging. That means he has some interest in Atencio. He and the warden don't get along either, so there might be something personal in this for him."

"Durant is a strange duck," Murrieta said. "Ambitious though he does not seem to know the law well. But you are right. He did not have to come this afternoon. What can he do?"

"Let's ask," Slocum said. He began shucking off the poorly fitting uniform, glad to once more be in his own clothes. As the cross-draw holster settled on his hip, he felt more confident. "Where's his office?"

"In San Francisco."

"He's not far ahead of us. We can overtake his buggy. Might be he wouldn't want anyone else around when I ask him to bribe a judge or buy off a guard or two."

"You would still break Atencio out?"

"If it comes to that. I'd rather Durant find a legal way of getting him free. A botched hanging might not be enough, but this gives us more time to bring the banker around to our way of thinking."

They rode hard and caught the lawyer as he was driving his buggy onto the ferry across the Golden Gate. Slocum tossed the reins of the horses to Murrieta and went to talk with Durant.

The lawyer looked up as Slocum approached, slid his hand under his coat, probably resting it on the butt of a pistol. He frowned when it became obvious Slocum was not going away.

"Whoever you are, I don't want to talk," Durant said.

"It's about Atencio, the man in San Quentin you went to see hanged."

Durant frowned even more and then said slowly, "I've seen you before. Where?"

"That's not important. We share a desire. Get your client out of prison."

"You were the guard who escorted me out."

"What do you need to free Atencio?" Slocum didn't want the lawyer thinking too much on why a guard was interested in freeing a prisoner.

"Money," Durant said without hesitation. "If I get enough, all things are possible." He snorted contemptuously. "Especially in this state. There's nothing that can't be bought."

"Including the warden?"

"Harriman'd never listen to me. He'd take too much pleasure throwing me in his darkest, deepest cell. No, there are others. Judges. Prosecutors."

"The banker who brought the charges?"

"Hez Galworthy might be bought off, but I'm not sure of that. What's your interest? You're not one of them."

"Them?"

"Murrieta's little family. That village he runs. If Atencio gets out, what's in it for you?"

"Justice," Slocum said. He had a strong dislike for seeing men railroaded for crimes they hadn't committed. From what he could tell, Murrieta and Maria were being honest when they said Atencio was innocent.

He didn't much trust bankers either.

"You have tried and failed at this," Maria said. "Why can you now find them?"

Slocum pursed his lips. He had gone over a dozen harebrained schemes since getting the stay of execution for Atencio using his knife on the rope, but none had produced any solid sense that they would work.

"I can find them," he said. "The Valenzuelas are still in the area. That means they don't think the law is on to them, and they might have other robberies in the works."

"So?" Maria shrugged her shapely shoulders.

"So we need money for the lawyer. Durant hinted that he could bribe somebody into letting Atencio go. The judge, the banker, who knows? I suspect he has an inside track to the judge. Galworthy isn't likely to go back on his testimony with Atencio so close to being hanged. That would make him look bad."

"You have a plan to find them again?"

The woman's barely concealed scorn stung him. Then he calmed down. She was right, and anything he did was likely to fail as it had before. Conchita had the sheriff's ear and could turn out a posse to chase him down whenever it suited her. If he got too close—or found their loot—she would have Bernard on his trail in two shakes of a lamb's tail.

"Wait and see," he said with more confidence than he felt. But he did have a way to find her. She was likely to be the one going into Miramar for supplies or to speak with Sheriff Bernard. José was an escaped prisoner, and their father wasn't likely to poke about town, even if he wasn't on his deathbed.

"Wait and see," Maria said, standing in front of him and lifting her peasant blouse to give him a flash of bare, nut brown breasts. And then she turned and hurried from the house. Slocum heaved a sigh. He knew what his reward would be. All it took was a bit of luck to claim it.

He went, saddled his horse, and rode down the road toward Miramar, then cut across country before he got within sight. The seacoast town brought a fair amount of traffic along the road through the coast hills that he wanted to avoid. If no one spotted him, nobody could tell the sheriff or a posse out combing the countryside.

When he found a spot on a rocky butte looking down at the road running through the center of town, he dismounted, got some jerky, and sat gnawing on it as he watched for Conchita. He knew it might be a long wait. If it stretched longer than a few days, Atencio would swing. Durant needed time to put the money to use, and Slocum had to believe a day or two might pass before he could even find where the Valenzuelas had stashed their ill-gotten gains.

Lounging back, propped on one elbow, he stared out

over the endless sea, feeling a kinship with its restlessness. Always moving, never the same when he looked back, the ocean might have been his calling if he hadn't grown up around horses on a farm. He preferred a sturdy horse under him and the vast plains or mountains stretching to the sky over the barren, always moving gunmetal gray ocean.

His mind drifted as he daydreamed about what life might be like with Maria. She was a fiery woman. But then he had wondered the same with Conchita, and she had used him to get her brother free from prison, then made sure the law would come down hard on him if he so much as showed his face. Conchita was a schemer, a planner, the competent crook. Not at all like Maria, she—

Slocum sat up, grabbed for a small spyglass he had brought along, and peered through it. He wanted to cry out in joy but held his delight in check. Conchita was riding from Miramar, heading east through the hills. Whether he had missed her going into town or she had been there before he had taken up watch didn't matter. She was leaving. The only place she was likely heading had to be her hideout.

He stepped up into the saddle, retraced his path to the butte, and found the road twenty minutes later. Conchita couldn't be more than a mile ahead of him, but she wouldn't remain on the road very long, he suspected. Riding faster, he came within a few hundred yards of her as he veered off the road and rode to a stand of trees.

Slocum recognized this as the spot where José and his father had run after the stagecoach robbery—and where Conchita had almost sicced the sheriff and his posse on him.

With more assurance now, he rode into the woods and felt the cool darkness wrap around him like a damp blanket. Through the spindly tree trunks he saw flashes of the woman ahead of him. When she cut suddenly to the right, he took a route parallel and began edging closer. By the time Conchita rode out into a draw that led to a peaceful meadow, he was close enough to attract her attention.

Jerking about when she heard his horse's hoofbeats, she reached for a six-shooter slung in a belt around her saddle horn. Slocum galloped forward, and as she raised the pistol to fire, he kicked free of the stirrups and sailed through the air. His arms circled her lithe body. Then his shoulder hit her side, and she was lifted from the saddle. Both of them tumbled to the ground, Slocum on top.

Conchita lay pinned under him, gasping for air. He reached out and snared the six-shooter in her limp fingers. This revitalized her, and she began kicking and clawing in earnest. He moved his knees to her shoulders and held her in a schoolboy pin so he could look down into her lovely face. There was no way around it. Conchita was about the most gorgeous woman he had ever seen, but that lovely face now contorted into ugly rage.

"I'll kill you!" she cried. "You cannot have me this way."

"I don't want you," he said. The words were like cold water in her face.

She looked at him, stunned.

"You do not want me? But . . ."

"I want my money for springing José from prison," he said. "You owe me. Money. And my pay just doubled."

"I will not—"

"I don't want you," Slocum said coldly. "I want my money. Pay me what's due, and I'll get out of your hair."

"We have no money."

"You've got plenty after robbing both the stage and the bank in Miramar."

Her eyes went wide with surprise. Conchita shook her head as if this would be denial enough. When she saw he wasn't going to believe her, she tried fighting him again. His weight proved too much for her to budge.

"You are hurting me," she said.

"Might be I'll do more than that if you try cheating me. You not only tried to steal what's my due, you put the sheriff on my trail and lied about me robbing the bank."

"The stage, too," she said, a wicked smile curling her lips. The beauty fled, replaced by pure evil.

"Clever. Now pay me."

"You will leave us alone?"

"I won't even be a memory, 'cept for how much I took."

"One hundred dollars."

"One thousand dollars."

"We do not have so much. We robbed the bank and stagecoach but took only a few dollars."

He couldn't forget the image of José gunning down the passengers on the stage or how their father had shot the driver until he was deader than a doornail.

"Let's go count it."

She glared sullenly at him, then nodded once. Slocum rolled to the side and let her get to her feet. She rubbed her shoulders where his knees had pinned her so securely.

"You bruised me. You are a vicious man, John Slocum."

He didn't answer. She read his expression and turned away to flounce toward her horse. Slocum caught up the reins on his and mounted to ride beside her. Conchita stared ahead, never even glancing at him out of the corner of her eye. The meadow wasn't too large, but a small stream ran through the center and vanished into the woods a hundred yards downhill.

"There," she said. "We are over there."

As Slocum turned to look in the direction she pointed, Conchita swung hard. Her tiny fist caught him on the cheek. The unexpected blow caused him to recoil and fight to keep in the saddle. By the time he had pulled himself back securely into the saddle, she had galloped straight ahead and disappeared into the woods. He started after her, then slowed and looked at the soft dirt on the ground and how the tufts of grass had been cut up from other horses passing by.

Conchita tried to lead him away from her real hideout. From the tracks, more than one horse had gone to a spot opposite where she had pointed. He trotted along this small trail. The riders hadn't tried to conceal their hoof-prints, telling him the Valenzuelas felt secure against be-ing tracked to this area.

He slid into a lightly wooded section and wended his way around, hunting for tracks in the leaves and pine nee-dle carpet. Finding the trail proved as easy as falling off a log. Slocum came to another clearing. A small cooking fire smoldered in the middle of the sward; a pot of coffee brewed and sent its aroma to his nostrils. He inhaled deeply. A cup wouldn't be amiss while he waited for them to come to him.

And they would. He had found them. Their cache had to be in the area, perhaps even in their camp.

Slocum dismounted and went to the fire. A pair of tin cups had been turned upside down on rocks next to the coffeepot, dangling from a tripod of green limbs over the fire. He poured himself some coffee and prowled around. Three bedrolls. No sign of their ill-gotten gains from the stage or bank.

And no trace of José or his father.

Slocum sipped at the coffee, ignoring how bitter it tasted on his tongue. It might have been the coffee or the memory of how Conchita had convinced him so easily that her pa was dying and this would be José's only chance to see him before he died.

Slocum drained the cup and went back to the fire for an-other. As he bent, he heard an asthmatic wheezing. Looking up, he saw an old man shuffling painfully from the forest, a rabbit in one hand and a rifle in the other.

"*¿Que tal, José?*" The old man shuffled closer.

Slocum stayed low by the fire but slid his Colt from his

holster. The old man came closer, squinting hard. He acted as if he was almost blind.

Slocum tossed the tin cup away to rattle against a rock a few feet to his left. The old man turned in the direction of the sound, dropped the rabbit he had bagged for dinner, and lifted his rifle. He got off a shot that came damned near the cup.

"You're dead if you don't drop that rifle," Slocum called. "Now!"

The elder Valenzuela started to turn back, rifle still tucked into his shoulder.

"I can see plenty good, and you're in my sights," Slocum said. "Drop the rifle, and I'll let you live."

"Slocum." The name came out in a snake's hiss. "Conchita said you were in jail."

"We need to talk about that," Slocum said. "The rifle. Now! Drop it now!"

The old man finally did as he was told. He threw the rifle down. Slocum flinched as it discharged from the impact, but he never wavered in keeping the man in his gun sight.

"Why do you not kill me?"

"Tell me where the gold you stole is hidden, and you can live."

"Kill me!"

Slocum considered doing just that, then knew there was a better use for this murderous old codger. He was arthritic and damned near blind, but he was a cold-blooded killer. Watching him during the stagecoach robbery had shown that. Nobody but his son and daughter would miss him if he ended up with a couple slugs in his belly.

But he was worth more alive than dead.

"We're going on a little ride. Where's your horse?"

The way Valenzuela turned betrayed the location of his horse just inside the woods. His horse was fastened to a single rope strung between two trees. Slocum had to saddle the horse for the old man, but that was small price to pay for his ticket to a passel of money.

He herded the old man away from camp at gunpoint, already counting the money his ransom would bring.

14

"He eats like a horse," Maria said, glaring at the old man.

Conchita's father shoveled food into his mouth as if he hadn't eaten in a month of Sundays. For all Slocum knew, that might be true. He didn't see either of the man's children being too generous with food or money.

He had to speak up over the click of a spoon against the tin plate as the man scooped a third helping of beans into his mouth, then wiped the plate clean with what remained of a tortilla. He looked up expectantly.

"I will not feed him any more," said Maria. She folded her arms across her chest and glared.

"Won't have to," Slocum said, opening his pocket watch and looking at the time. "They know he's gone by now and have read my ransom note."

"They will not pay for me," the elder Valenzuela said. He spit. "They are not good children. They use me!"

"They wouldn't let him go," Slocum said to reassure himself as much as Maria and Procipio Murrieta, who stood in the doorway watching over them like a hawk circling prey. "He protests, but he's the reason they had me break José out of San Quentin. He means more to them than he's letting on."

"More food?" The old man held out his plate. "*¿Más comida?*"

"Go to hell," Maria said, grabbing the plate from him and flinging it across the room to smash into the far wall. She spun and faced Slocum. "This is a crazy plan. They will not pay. Atencio will die because of the time we waste with this . . . *viejo!*"

"How else do you get him out of prison? Atencio got a stay of execution for a week. If the lawyer can find the right palm to grease, he might get Atencio out. I don't see any other way of saving him from the noose."

"They would commute the death sentence," Murrieta said. "He would still be in prison."

"That's better than being in the prison cemetery," Slocum said. He had caught a glimpse of it outside the wall. Considering the warden's predilection for ceremony and keeping dissent down, he was surprised it wasn't within the walls where prisoners could see what happened if they misbehaved.

"You give them too much time to scheme. They will kill you and steal back this . . . this . . ." Maria sputtered, unable to find the words to describe her unwilling guest.

"I looked around the campsite and didn't see where they could have hidden the loot. They probably stashed it far enough away to be safe from casual discovery but close enough so they could get it when they wanted. It wouldn't be more than an hour's ride."

"They will double-cross you," Maria insisted.

Slocum only nodded. He expected them to. The Valenzuelas were as slippery as eels and had the table manners of a famished grizzly. He had to be slicker, meaner, and sharper. Anticipating their every move was difficult because they might decide their welcome in northern California was worn out and just move on, leaving their pa behind. However, Slocum doubted that would happen. They were a tight-knit family and the old man sitting at the table, hands folded peacefully across the spot where his plate had rested only minutes earlier, had the look of a patriarch. José and Conchita might have the fire, but the old man had the cunning.

Slocum decided that Conchita was truly the old man's daughter and had inherited her own cozening ways honestly.

"You sure about the canyon?" Slocum asked Murrieta, who only shrugged and looked impassive. "Let's ride."

He grabbed Valenzuela by the bony shoulder and lifted him from the chair. The old man was skin and bones and winced at the pressure. Slocum didn't care. For what the Valenzuela family had done to him, he would as soon gun them all down. Memory of how this seemingly fragile, almost blind man had murdered the stagecoach driver burned brightly, too. Given the chance, any of the Valenzuelas would kill without remorse.

He could match them.

Outside he got the old man onto a horse and led him along. Murrieta held back, as if he intended to stay in the village and let Slocum do the dirty work. Slocum rubbed his gun hand on his thigh to make sure it was dry. Letting his six-shooter slip when he needed it most was a sure way to end up dead and forgotten.

Or would Maria forget him so easily?

"Why do you do this? Who are you?" Valenzuela asked. Slocum didn't bother answering. Being distracted could only lead to mistakes.

Slocum let the old man natter on, commenting on this and that and occasionally going on about how loyal his daughter and son were but how they wouldn't pay good money for a decrepit pile of bones. This convinced Slocum he had something worth trading. There wasn't any reason to deny his worth if the old man really thought he was worthless.

The narrow canyon mouth made Slocum reconsider the wisdom of his plan. Then he knew it had to be done this way or he'd never get money from the Valenzuelas. He rode to the spot Murrieta had suggested and looked around. A small pool of water bubbled from the ground. Bones of small animals told of the poison in the water.

"I'm thirsty. Let me drink."

"Go on," Slocum said. He kept a sharp eye on the surrounding countryside. There were too many spots where a sniper might bushwhack him, so he decided to force the Valenzuelas' hand. And he did. The old man dropped to his belly and started to drink.

"*¡Tomé no, Papa!*"

José rose from behind a tangle of undergrowth not ten feet away. Slocum hadn't seen him. He reckoned Conchita was hidden somewhere else. If they thought it necessary, there would be others, also.

"I'd listen to him," Slocum advised. "That pond's poison. *Venenoso.*"

José's father looked up. The sly look on his face told Slocum that age hadn't dimmed the man's brain. He had done this to fake being ill, thinking to gain an advantage. The hardness that came to his eyes showed that Slocum would have died if he had tried to save the old man and had, even for an instant through carelessness, lost his six-gun.

"Come here, Papa," José called. "I have him covered."

"You want to lose him?" Slocum slid his six-shooter from its holster and aimed it at the prone man's back. "You shoot me, I kill him. He's not spry enough to get away."

"You would trade your life for him?" José sounded amazed at this.

"No, since I expect you to give me the thousand dollars

I asked for. I'll take the money and ride off. Your pa stays where he is in my gun sight until I see the gold."

José Valenzuela shifted, as if trying to decide which he was willing to lose, his father or the money. Slocum knew how the playacting would end but still kept his pistol aimed at the elder Valenzuela.

"I will do as you say, but I will track you to the ends of the world if you harm him."

"The money," Slocum said coldly.

José disappeared, then popped back up like a prairie dog. He held a canvas bag in his hand.

"Show me the money. Open the bag, and show me what's inside."

Valenzuela glared, then put down his rifle and fumbled to open the mouth of the bag. He opened it and held it out for Slocum to see inside. Slocum cocked his six-shooter to indicate what he wanted next. He could either shoot the helpless old man or José could reach into the bag and show its contents.

With ill grace, José pulled out a couple handfuls of scrip.

"Where's the gold?"

"There was none," José said. "Only this paper money."

"Toss out your rifle, then the money bag."

"You will kill both my papa and me."

"The thought's crossed my mind," Slocum said, "but it'd be a waste of bullets—if there's enough money in that bag."

"It is all we stole."

Slocum snorted in contempt at the obvious lie. The bank had lost a fair amount of gold coin because Galworthy had complained about the loss to Sheriff Bernard. Although the banker might have lied, there was little reason for him to have done so unless he had been stealing from his own bank. Since he was the owner and president, that seemed unlikely. Galworthy robbed legally from everyone in the county and could keep his racket going for years to come. His depositors were not likely to look kindly on him if he didn't make good any losses on their part.

"Here." Valenzuela swung the bag around his head in a wide circle and released it. The canvas bag sailed through the air and landed near the poisoned pond.

"Pick it up, and give it to me," Slocum told José's father. The man stood painfully, hefted the bag, and made a big show of how heavy it was.

Slocum grabbed it from his hand and peered inside, rooting around. He wasn't sure how much was inside, but it wasn't a thousand dollars. He hadn't expected that much. The Valenzuelas kept as much as they gave—probably more.

"Go on over to your son."

He kept his pistol trained on the man's back as he shuffled to where José stood. When the elder Valenzuela crossed in front of José, Slocum put his heels to his horse's flanks and galloped away. José retrieved his rifle and got off a couple shots that went high and wide. This alerted Slocum that they had something more in store for him than a bullet in the back.

Securing the bag with the name of the stagecoach company stenciled in smeary black ink on the canvas, he rode back toward the canyon mouth, hunting for the landmarks Murrieta had given him. He saw the twin trees with the lightning-struck stump and immediately to the left the faint trail. Losing himself in the wooded area, he continued to ride for the canyon wall. Other markers assured him he was on the correct path and that Murrieta had a good memory for trail markers.

He forced his horse through a narrow defile that widened to a rocky path hardly wide enough for his horse. Slocum dismounted and led the horse up the side of the canyon. The twisting and turning trail hid him often from the canyon floor, but when he came to the canyon rim, he stopped and looked down.

A smile came to his lips. He recognized Conchita immediately, gesturing frantically. Even at this distance she was one hell of a beautiful woman, but he guessed what her expression would be. All twisted up in a mask of fury and hatred. Her words would tell of the worst outlaw ever to ride on California dirt.

And listening to her was Sheriff Bernard with four deputies.

The Valenzuelas had sacrificed some of their loot to put Slocum's head in a noose. Sheriff Bernard and his posse would capture a real desperado in the narrow canyon along with proof that he had robbed the stage and probably the Miramar bank. They would have their pa back and be rid of Slocum once and for all.

Slocum laughed. He had expected something like this. While he hadn't known what the Valenzuelas would pull, they were as crooked as a dog's hind leg and as cunning as any hungry wolf. Stepping up into the saddle, Slocum followed the ridge until he found another marker where Murrieta had said, then worked his way down into the canyon beyond. From there it took him less than an hour to return to the village with the money needed to free Atencio.

"It worked? It worked!" Maria threw her arms around his neck and kissed him soundly. If Murrieta hadn't been there watching, Slocum would have explored how far the woman's gratitude ran. Still, he kissed her longer than was good for her reputation before pushing her away.

Maria's dark eyes glowed with admiration. He had to compare this with how he guessed Conchita Valenzuela's had flared when she set the sheriff on his trail in an otherwise clever trap.

"I have heard from friends in Miramar," Murrieta said. "The sheriff is angry with Conchita for leading him on this wild-goose chase. He ordered her away."

"Maybe now he'll stop listening to her," Slocum said. "That'll make my life easier." He shuffled the stacks of bills around on the table. "I ought to have known better than to think they'd hand over very much. There's hardly two hundred dollars here."

"It will be enough?" Maria's eagerness dampened Slocum's triumph a little.

"Can't say. Depends on what Durant can do with it. Will any judge be bribed for two hundred dollars in greenbacks?"

"Judge Ralston might. He gambles often but not well," Maria said. She clung to Slocum's arm. "What if we need more?"

"That'll be up to your lawyer to let us know. Might be this kind of money would bribe a guard at the prison." Slocum felt the bile rise and burn at the back of his throat. Having any further dealings around San Quentin gave him the collywobbles. He wanted nothing more than to be done with this, Atencio free, and him on the road to Oregon or just about anywhere else.

"Procipio has sent for him. He will be here soon."

Slocum started to suggest a way to spend the time before the lawyer arrived when he heard a buggy rattling along the rocky road leading into the village. He scooped up the bills and tucked them into his coat pocket. Letting a lawyer see money before things got spelled out was always a mistake. They focused on the money and nothing more.

Slocum laughed wryly. In some ways, lawyers and the Valenzuela family were alike. Dangle money in front of them and they looked for the most devious way possible to grab it.

"I'm a busy man. This had better be good, Murrieta."

Durant pushed past Procipio and stood in the small room looking belligerent.

"How are you coming with getting Atencio out of prison?" Slocum asked. Durant was a busy man. He said so. There was no need for pleasantries—or politeness.

"I can't find a judge to issue a longer stay of execution or to go along with the idea that he's been hanged once so he can't be hanged twice for the same crime."

"What about getting the banker to say he was wrong identifying Atencio as a horse thief?"

Durant waved his hand about, as if shooing away horse-flies.

"Galworthy is too caught up in putting a new vault in his bank. He's tired of getting robbed, he says. Doesn't say a thing about how he robs anyone who puts money in or those he loans to."

"So you've given up trying?" Slocum winced as Maria's fingernails cut into his arm. She wanted to blurt out her anger but instead clawed at his arm, letting him do the talking.

"There's only so much I can do, and everyone is starting to ridicule me. There wasn't any evidence against Atencio save that of the banker's eyewitness testimony. Galworthy's come out and said all you people look the same to him." Durant stared at Maria, putting the lie to that. "A man shot up the bank, broke the window, and then took Galworthy's own horse and rode away."

"Galworthy only saw the horse thief from behind?" Slocum asked.

"I tried to bring that out in the trial, but the judge wouldn't let the jury hear it. Banker Hezekiah Galworthy is a fine, upstanding man and pillar of the community so if he said Atencio stole a horse, that was good enough."

"He was not even in Miramar when this happened," Maria said, finally unable to contain herself. "He was here. In this village."

"Out in the fields working?" asked Durant.

"No," Maria said reluctantly. "He was in bed."

"So he was too sick to even be in Miramar," Slocum said. "There weren't any other witnesses?"

"None. And Galworthy and Atencio were feuding. The animosity stretched back a month or more over payment on his mortgage. Everybody knew that." Durant heaved a shuddery sigh. "I can't get elected dog catcher after this. My career is damned near at an end."

"Can you bribe a judge?" Slocum asked 'flat out when he saw Durant begin to shift his weight from one foot to the other, getting ready to leave.

"That's highly irregular, not to mention illegal."

"How much would it take to get Atencio's sentence commuted?" Slocum watched the lawyer closely.

Durant looked from Slocum to Murrieta blocking the doorway, then back. He rubbed his hands on the sides of his coat. Slocum didn't see the outline of a six-gun or smaller pistol, though the lawyer obviously wanted a weapon in his hands right about now.

"I don't know. That's something you have to edge around. Invite them for a drink. Feel out their needs."

"Heard tell Judge Ralston has big gambling losses." Slocum pulled out the wad of greenbacks and put them on the table in front of him where Durant could see.

The lawyer licked his lips, rubbed his hands some more, and finally came to some sort of a decision. From the way the man's face went blank, Slocum knew playing poker with Durant would be a sure way to lose. For all his nervousness before, he was dead calm now and unreadable.

"There might be a tad of truth in that," Durant said. "After a drink or two he becomes, shall we say, aggressive in his betting. That aggression is seldom coupled with luck. Or skill."

Slocum held up the stack of bills, riffled through them,

then held them out. Durant made the greenbacks disappear as if by magic.

"It might take a few days for me to put this money to good use."

"Don't go taking too long," Slocum said. "Atencio is due to swing real soon."

"Yes, there is that," Durant said. "I'll do what I have to for him."

"You'll get him out," Slocum said, an edge coming to his voice.

"Sir, that might not be possible. For this amount of money, stopping the hanging might be the full extent of what I can do. Better to be sentenced to life in San Quentin than to die within those walls."

"No!" Maria cried out and started around the table. Slocum stopped her with an arm around her waist.

"Let him do what he can. If Atencio's sentence is changed, we can work on a pardon later."

"Yes, that's right," Durant said, his face still an emotionless mask. "There'll be all the time in the world then."

The lawyer nodded brusquely, pushed past Murrieta, and in a few minutes the clatter of his buggy along the rocky road disappeared, leaving only the normal sounds of the farming village behind.

"All we can do is wait," Slocum told Maria and Murrieta. The words tasted like ash on his tongue. He wasn't one for waiting. He wanted to be doing something, but for once he had to let someone else do the work even if he didn't like it.

15

"He is gone," cried Procipio Murrieta. "I have looked, others have sought him, but he is gone!"

"What are you talking about?" Slocum had the cold knot in his gut that he knew what Murrieta was saying but needed to hear it spelled out.

"Durant has taken the money and left. He sold his buggy and horse, took the ferry to Oakland, and is gone!"

"Son of a bitch," Slocum muttered. He ground his teeth together as he let anger wash over him. Never trust a shyster. By now he ought to know that and yet had let Durant waltz away with the money that might have sprung Atencio from prison if they had bribed a guard. Now they had nothing, and Atencio again was due to hang in two days.

"We should never have trusted him," Murrieta said.

"He was your lawyer," Slocum pointed out. He immediately regretted having spoken. It wasn't Murrieta's fault. It was Durant's for being a slimy maggot. By now, Durant could be a hundred miles away. More. He could have caught a train and be on the other side of the Sierras by now, far out of reach of retribution for his theft.

"There is no chance he goes there to find a way to free Atencio?" Maria asked. She had been working in the field and was covered with fresh earth.

"Gomez told me of the sale of the buggy and horse. Durant said he had important business back East."

"He might have needed the money to add to what John gave him," Maria said.

She fell silent when she saw the expressions on Murrieta's and Slocum's faces.

"How do you get him out?" Murrieta asked.

Slocum had no answer. San Quentin was a fortress filled with guards. He had sneaked in once as a prisoner and another time as a guard. There wasn't any way in hell he'd try either of those subterfuges again. Unable to pace as he thought, he left the small house and went out into the bright sunlight. A few white clouds worked their way in from over the ocean. Otherwise nothing disturbed the broad blue expanse overhead. A few seagulls vented their wrath at not having enough to eat—they never got enough.

They never got enough rattled over and over in Slocum's head. He had to stop now. If he kept on, he would not only fail to free Atencio but would end up a prisoner again. It didn't matter if Wilkinson locked him up as Jasper Jarvis or John Slocum. To be in San Quentin again would mean his eventual death.

"John, where are you going?" Maria came from the house, wiping her hands on a rag.

"I need to think."

"Of ways to free Atencio?"

She recoiled at his black look. He began walking, not sure where he went but wanting to be away from the village and all its hardworking men and women. They struggled to grow their beans and wanted nothing more than to live quietly, raise families, and . . .

And not be locked up in San Quentin on trumped-up charges.

He came to a path leading to the top of a low hill. He trooped to the summit and then sat on a rock, staring across the cultivated fields. Some were brown from lack of irrigation but many were producing good crops. He remembered his home in Calhoun, Georgia, and how the family had farmed. Grains, mostly, and alfalfa for the livestock. Those had been good days before the war.

His family was long dead. He pulled his watch from his vest pocket and looked at it, case closed. This was his only legacy from his brother, Robert. Robert had been the good hunter. Slocum had tried to match his accuracy and stealthiness and had usually come up shy of that ideal. Robert had died during Pickett's Charge. All the marksmanship and woodsmanship in the world wouldn't have saved him once he started marching into the Federal guns.

Slocum wasn't going to keep barking up the tree— the tree where Atencio would be hanged. He didn't know the man and only owed Murrieta the effort to get his friend free from San Quentin because of how he had sacrificed himself in the first escape. There had to be an end, and Slocum had reached it.

He went into a crouch and had his Colt out of the holster at the faint crunch of a foot turning a rock behind him.

"You are very fast," Maria said. "Your aim is good also, I suspect."

"You shouldn't have followed."

"I had to, John, I had to. Atencio means the world to me, to Procipio, to the entire village." She moved forward, as silent as a ghost now. He wondered if her tiny feet ever touched the earth. She had cleaned up and put on a fresh blouse. Her billowing skirt needed serious cleaning after her work in the fields, but he suspected she did not have another. Not for everyday use. He was sure she had a fancy Sunday-go-to-meeting dress, but there was no call for such wear now.

"I've done all I can. I can track down Durant and try to get the money back, but time's running out."

"Two days," she said sadly. Maria moved closer and reached out to touch his cheek. "You have done all you could. I am sure Procipio will release you from your promise."

That stung him. He jerked away and stared out over the valley and its neat fields of growing pinto beans. Some men made promises and forgot them right away. Slocum kept his. Having Maria tell him Murrieta would relieve him of his word, freely given, burned like a knife wound in his gut.

"What else can I do?"

"There is nothing," she said. "You are so very clever to have saved Atencio. But you are going?"

"Yes." He saw no reason to lie. Breaking his promise was bad enough.

"It is for the best. The sheriff hunts you, the guards from San Quentin seek you out, and even the Valenzuelas would kill you if they find you. There is no one here to keep you safe."

Maria moved closer. Her lush body pressed into his back as her arms circled his waist and held him close. He found it increasingly difficult to simply stand. Her fingers pressed lower, beneath the buckle of his gun belt, moving slowly, carefully, stimulating and making him increasingly uncomfortable trapped in his jeans.

Slocum gasped when she unfastened his gun belt and let it drop to the ground, then began working on the buttons holding his fly together. When he sprang free, warm air surrounding his rigid manhood, he sighed with relief. Then he gasped again as her fingers circled him and began exerting a steady pressure all around. The warmth of her hand, the way she knew exactly where to touch him, made Slocum steely hard.

He ran his hands back along hers, up her wrists, and

stroked her bare forearms. She pressed her cheek against his back. He felt her soft breathing become increasingly harsh as she moved her body against his.

He turned slowly in the circle of her arms. He was reluctant to have her release her hold on him but knew there was more, better, waiting. He kissed her upturned face. Her lips, her eyes, down to a shell-like ear. His tongue lightly ran around the rim. Maria sighed with the feathery light touch.

Slocum groaned as he felt her hands return to work on his erection again.

Continuing to pioneer his trail of wet kisses, he followed her jaw and went to her slender throat. From there he burrowed lower, popping open the crisp white blouse and finding the nut-colored breasts waiting so enticingly for him. He sucked one nipple into his mouth and tongued it. This produced a heartfelt moan of desire. He quickly left that nipple and went to the other. After giving it the same treatment, he buried his face between her breasts. The warm, sleek flesh on either side of his face aroused him. He worked lower.

"Oh, yes, John, I want you so!"

He slid his hands up under her skirts and began lifting. Her flesh slipped like satin under his fingers as he worked upward. Her calves, her thighs, inside those luscious things. Higher. She cried out when he slid a finger into her wet slit. Working it around in the tightness, he caused her to almost lose her balance. He was on his knees as he fingered her. She had to balance by putting her hands on his shoulders.

With a surge up, he stood and pressed his hips forward. The plum-tipped throbbing organ between his legs found the perfect fit between her. Where his finger had been in an instant before, he now drove upward. Surrounded by her tightness, her heat, her sexual vibrancy, he lifted her onto her toes. It took him but a second to wrap his arms around her waist and hoist her up entirely.

Her legs parted, then circled about his waist so they hung together as one. For a long minute, neither breathed, neither moved. Then Maria's hips began a slow gyration. She pressed down, moved in a slow, erotic circle, and pulled back just enough. Slocum felt as if he was being crushed by her strong inner muscles.

Kissing her as she moved drove both their desires higher. His hands cupped her rump, then began bouncing her up and down to match the circular movement she provided. The combination of in-out and up-down caused a prairie fire to rage in his loins.

He spun about and caught sight of the farms spread below. The wind whipping off those fields cooled the sweat beading on his forehead and plastering his shirt to his body. The combination of hot and cold caused his passions to bubble even more. With a quick move, he dropped to his knees and leaned forward so Maria was flat on her back, her legs still up in the air.

In this position he had better leverage. His thrusts grew in power. Each drove deeper into her willing, wanton body. She gasped and thrashed about as she clawed at his upper arms. Her dark eyes popped open, but they were glazed with lust.

"Yes, yes," she sobbed out.

Slocum moved faster but could not maintain the steady rhythm. His own desire passed the point of no return. His movement became jerky, hard, deep. And then he exploded within her core.

Her back arched and she rammed her crotch down hard into his to take every inch of him she could. And then they sank down together, lying side by side. Their desires were sated, and both had no words.

They held each other, Maria with her head resting on his chest. He felt her hot breath again, but this time it was slow, even.

He stroked her lustrous black hair and felt her snuggle

even closer. Looking past her, he saw the sky was filling with puffy white clouds. There might be rain later, but he doubted it. The season was dry.

Dry. Was it so lacking that it would never rain again? Was he so lacking in honor that he would not keep a promise he had made?

"I'll think of something," he said softly.

"I know," Maria answered.

Neither moved until the sun began to set, then they returned to the village. When they spent the night together in Maria's tiny bed, he still had no idea how to rescue Atencio from the gallows.

16

"The sheriff comes," Maria whispered. "Hide, John, or he will see you!"

Slocum pressed back against the gunsmith's shop in Miramar, just down the street from the sheriff's office. He knew the risk he took coming to town but had no other choice. Time pressed down on him something fierce, with Atencio scheduled for execution tomorrow morning.

"I need those supplies," he told her, keeping his head down to hide his face under his broad hat brim.

"You will be in jail. Here he comes!"

"Decoy him. If I try to go now, he'll spot me for sure." Slocum settled down in a chair, rocked back, and pulled his hat even lower over his face. He heard the sheriff's boots clicking on the boardwalk as he approached. From the corner of his eye, he saw the lawman's feet come and stop just inches away. Slocum fancied he could feel Bernard's breath gusting against the crown of his hat. It took all his control not to go for his six-shooter.

"I know you," Sheriff Bernard said.

"I am from the farming village outside town," Maria said.

"You hang around with Procipio Murrieta, don't you?"

"I have not seen him."

"Didn't ask that. 'Course you haven't seen him since he's an escaped prisoner from San Quentin."

"He is our *alcalde*."

"He does keep the peace out yonder," Bernard said. "I appreciate that since I got my hands full around town. Around the rest of the county, too." The sheriff spit into the street and continued, "He won't have any problem with me. I don't cotton much to those folks up at San Quentin. If Murrieta keeps his nose clean around here, I just won't see him. If you get what I mean."

Slocum wanted to twitch, to scratch his nose, to move, but he held back. Any move on his part would bring the sheriff's attention to him. The last thing he wanted was to gun down the lawman.

"You do not pursue him?"

"Got bigger fish to fry. Let that blowhard from San Quentin retrieve his own damn prisoners." Bernard coughed and said, "Sorry, ma'am, didn't mean to say that, but Sergeant Wilkinson gets my danger up faster 'n 'bout anyone else in these parts. Don't know for certain sure but I think he broke out my prisoner and then shot up the jail."

"He is one of the prison guards?"

"You know he is. You been up there yourself to visit the man getting himself hanged tomorrow. Are you going to witness the execution?"

"No," Maria said in a tiny voice Slocum could hardly make out.

"Well, ma'am, then it'll be up to me to be a witness. Seems there was some mistake made before, and they made a botch of it, but you know that, don't you?"

"You mean to torment me with this talk, Sheriff."

"Ma'am, that's the farthest thing from my mind. Wish I could say I was just passing time with a lovely lady, but you know better." The boots shuffled away and the clicking went to Slocum's right side, then stopped. He imagined Bernard drawing his six-gun and pointing it right at his head as he said, "Now, ma'am, you haven't seen that Jarvis fellow around, have you? Wilkinson wants him, but I want him, too, especially since he's the one Wilkinson busted out of *my* jail. That riled me something fierce."

"Jarvis?"

"Jasper Jarvis is his cognomen. He robbed the stage and murdered all the folks on it. Now, I'd think a cold-blooded killer and road agent like that'd be two states over, but I keep getting reports of him in the area. A kidnapping, how he's planning more bedevilment. You haven't seen him, have you?"

"There is a fight starting in the saloon, Sheriff," Maria said.

"Is there now?" Bernard cleared his throat, spit again, and then said, "You don't stick that purty nose of yours poked into anyplace where it doesn't belong, now. Hear?"

Slocum chanced a quick glimpse from under his hat. Sheriff Bernard stalked off toward the saloon, where a fight had spilled out into the street. It was hardly 8 a.m. and already the brawling had begun in town.

"Did he suspect?" Slocum asked.

"I do not think he did, John," she said, moving to inter-pose her body between the retreating lawman and Slocum. "He would have tried to capture you if he had."

Slocum considered this and decided Maria was right. Bernard wasn't the sort to pussyfoot around. Cautiously letting down the chair legs, he got to his feet and turned his back to the sheriff, still walking slowly toward the saloon and sizing up the trouble. Maria trailed him.

"I need those supplies, but you see what I do?"

"Her," Maria said, making a sound like an angry cat. She started around Slocum but he caught her arm and held her back.

"Conchita is in town for some reason." His mind raced. "I've got to trail her so I can find José."

"She is—"

"This will keep Procipio safe."

"What? I don't understand."

"He volunteered to act as bait to get the San Quentin gates open and some of the guards outside. As an escaped prisoner, Wilkinson wants to grab him again. This is how we were going to get inside."

"Procipio would sacrifice himself in such a way?"

"For Atencio, he would. That's got to be a mighty special gent for so many of you to risk your lives to save his."

"Very special," Maria said softly. A catch made her next words unintelligible.

"You get all this," Slocum said, pulling a list with the items he needed scratched on it.

"I have so little money. How?"

"That's up to you, but if you don't get everything back to the village for Murrieta to get packed, we won't be able to get Atencio free."

"I will do this for you." Maria clutched the scrap of paper so hard she crumpled it. As she started away, Slocum caught her arm and swung her around.

For a moment they stared into each other's eyes. Then he kissed her.

"Get going," he said. "I'll see you in the village when I can."

Maria looked impish and grabbed him, giving him another kiss, one laced with promise. Then she laughed and rushed away toward the general store across the street. Slocum licked his lips and savored again the taste of the woman. Then he slipped into an alley and went toward the back of the buildings facing the street. He had guessed right. Conchita Valenzuela had tethered her horse behind the photographic studio.

She hurried from the rear door, looked around, then stepped up into the saddle. Without a seeming care in the world, Conchita rode away, heading to the road leading north out of town. Slocum took a deep breath, then fetched his own horse. He patted the stolen animal on the neck, then vaulted up and snapped the reins, trotting after Conchita. Coming to Miramar had been dangerous but was the only place Slocum had a chance of finding either Conchita or her brother.

And he needed her brother in a bad way. Real quick.

Conchita made no effort to hide her trail or avoid others on the road. She waved brightly to other travelers along the road, but Slocum hung back when she stopped greeting them and became more fixed on hunting for landmarks along the road. He was ready when she cut off the road and rode down into a ravine.

Standing in the stirrups, he got a sense where the ravine headed and galloped along to find a spot where the banks might have caved in so he could take this low road. Instead he found where Conchita left. She urged her horse up the far bank, then took a steep, gravelly incline and disappeared into low hills covered with soft grasses and low bushes.

Slocum pulled down the brim of his hat to keep the sun from distracting him as he carefully studied the entire hillside, especially the ridge running away. Anyone watching Conchita's back trail would outline himself against the blue sky. Seeing no one, he worked his way down into the ravine and up the other side, following the woman's tracks easily.

For an hour he tracked her, avoiding being seen. He often stopped to study the valley where she rode, watchful for her brother. The old man wasn't likely to be posted as lookout with his bad eyes, but Slocum worried about José.

He needn't have. At the far end of the peaceful valley with lush tufts of grass everywhere that tempted his horse, he saw a thin curl of smoke making its way into the afternoon sky. He had found the Valenzuelas' new campsite.

Cutting into the woods, he approached until his nostrils flared with the pungent scent of wood smoke. He wasn't too far off. Kicking his leg over the saddle, he dropped to the ground, considered taking his rifle, then decided his Colt was adequate for what needed to be done. As stealthily as any Apache, he came within a few feet of the dilapidated cabin that must have once belonged to a shepherd who'd tended his flock.

The rapid-fire Spanish coming from inside the cabin slowed his advance. Crouched low, he went to the back wall and pressed his eye against the rough wood until he found a chink that allowed him to peer inside. At first he wasn't sure what he saw, then realized Conchita was sitting with her back to the hole. When she moved, he caught sight of José at a table. His sister joined him at the table.

"We need more," she said irritably. "You gave away too much to Slocum."

"He would have killed papa if I hadn't," protested José.

"But so much!"

Slocum scowled. The greedy bitch begrudged even two hundred dollars for her father?

"The sheriff was supposed to catch him with the money. We would have been able to steal it back. Bernard would have locked it in his desk." José made a dismissive gesture. "Stealing from a locked desk is easier than from a bank vault."

"But a thousand dollars!"

"That is what he demanded. Isn't papa worth that much?" José leaned forward and took his sister's hands in his. She pulled away and half turned. Slocum froze because she stared directly at him—at the crack in the wall.

When she looked back at her brother, Slocum relaxed

and had to marvel at what a bunch of road agents this family was. José had cheated his own sister out of eight hundred dollars. And he looked good in his pa's eyes for paying so much in the exchange.

"I love him, but is he worth it? All he does is sleep and eat." Conchita pointed in the direction of a corner where Slocum couldn't see. The *viejo* must have been asleep.

"At least they fed him," José said.

"An expensive meal, if you ask me."

"Very well. We can do *one* more robbery," José said in resignation. "The stagecoach is too heavily guarded now. There is nothing left in the bank. What else can we rob?"

"There is plenty in San Francisco," she said.

"The police! They are everywhere, they are monsters! If we failed, they would beat us within an inch of our lives, then put us into their terrible jail."

"Then we don't fail. I have an idea which will serve us well. At the Palace Hotel tomorrow night is a big society dance. The richest of *los ricos* will be there. We steal a few necklaces, a wallet or two, take what we can, and then leave."

"We steal from all?"

"Fool," snapped Conchita. "We take what we can. It will be plenty, more than the pitiful few coins from the bank, more than the greenbacks from the stage. We rob them, then we go immediately to the ferry and cross to Oakland. From there we can go anywhere we please."

"What of the gold we have?"

Conchita pursed her lips. Slocum had to move about to get a better look at her face. She was in silhouette and utterly lovely. He was reminded anew how he had fallen under her spell.

"We must trust Papa," she said finally. "We give him everything. Put it on a pack animal, in saddlebags, however it is most easily carried. He can find his way to the ferry and wait for us on the other side."

"Why not send him now? He can get a hotel room to wait."

"A good idea, José," she said, taking his hands now and stroking them. "If we find ourselves hurried by the police, dealing with him would slow us. Yes, we can send him ahead. It might be good to have a place to hide if pursuit is greater than I expect it to be."

"Now?"

Conchita shrugged, then said, "We should. I will take him to the stash and send him on his way. I will meet you in Portsmouth Square tomorrow at sundown. That will give us time to prepare. Bring all our guns."

"This will be dangerous, *hermana*."

"Without risk, there can be no gain. Help me rouse him. I want to get started right away."

Slocum turned and pressed his back against the wall as he listened to them awaken their pa, get him dressed and out the door. An itchy feeling worked on him as he heard Conchita and her father ride away . . . to the stash where they had hidden everything they had stolen. Gold coins, scrip, all of it. If he got the drop on Conchita when she dug up the money, he could ride away and be rich—or at least well paid for all he had been through.

But there was Atencio. And Maria. And the promise he had given Murrieta. And Maria. That single name echoed in his head. She would hate him forever if he cut and ran now.

No amount of money would erase the festering sore in his conscience should he break his word to her.

He glanced around the side of the cabin. Conchita and her pa were gone, out of sight, on their way to get everything the Valenzuelas had stolen. His Colt Navy slid easily from his holster and felt comforting in his hand. He rounded the corner and jerked away as José unexpectedly came from inside.

For an instant both of them froze. José started for the six-shooter in his belt but Slocum already had his drawn.

"I'll drop you where you stand. Don't. Don't throw down on me. You'll be a dead man before you touch the butt."

"You turn up at the worst possible times," José said. "If you are here to kidnap the old man again, you are out of luck. He is gone."

"I found the one I want."

"I will not tell you where we have hidden our money."

"Good," Slocum said, smiling wolfishly. He enjoyed the way the man's face drained of blood. He thought he was going to die. After torture. "I just wanted another hostage."

José stared at Slocum, then laughed until tears came to his eyes.

"You will ransom *me*? As you did my papa? Who is to pay? Conchita? She will let me die."

"You know your sister better 'n anyone else, I reckon," Slocum said. "But I'm not ransoming you to her."

"No? Then what . . ." José's eyes went wide when he realized what Slocum intended. He went for the six-gun thrust into the waistband of his jeans.

17

José Valenzuela moved fast, but Slocum was faster. He squeezed off a round that tore through the man's shoulder, knocking him backward. Valenzuela took a step, caught his heel, and then his legs turned to jelly. He sat hard, the pistol falling from his nerveless right hand. For a moment, he remained motionless, stunned. He shook himself as if to get his senses back and reached for his fallen six-shooter.

Slocum stepped on his left wrist until he felt bones grating together.

"Stop! You are hurting me!"

Slocum eased up on the pressure, then kicked the gun away. He kept his own pointed straight at the sitting man.

"You've got a vivid imagination," Slocum told him. "What do you think I'm going to do with you?"

"I cannot return to that terrible place."

Slocum grinned ear to ear. It gave him considerable pleasure to know that others felt the same as he did about San Quentin and that he could inflict this much misery on Valenzuela. He wished he could substitute him for Atencio, but there was no way that'd happen. He'd have to be content with carrying through the plan that still boiled about foglike and nebulous in his head.

He reached down and grabbed the front of José's shirt. A powerful tug got the man onto his feet. In ten minutes they were mounted and riding north.

"You have become a bounty hunter?" Valenzuela asked.

"Nothing like that," Slocum said. He didn't cotton much to bounty hunters, but he cottoned even less to conversation right now. Too much had to go just right for Atencio to escape the noose again. Worthless talk would only slow him down in his single-minded drive to get to the stone-walled prison.

"I will cry out when we ride through San Francisco," Valenzuela said. "Better to die with a bullet than to—"

He sagged as Slocum rode closer and swung the long barrel of his six-gun with great precision. He clipped Valenzuela just above the ear. A tiny cut appeared, but the shock scrambled brains and turned his grip on consciousness slippery.

Slocum had to support him as they rode the streets of San Francisco, heading north to where the ferry embarked to cross the Golden Gate from just east of Fort Point. The grim fortress that had protected the entrance to the Bay during the war bristled with cannons. A few bluecoats paraded back and forth along the ramparts, keeping watch for who knew what. There had never been a threat to the city during the war, and even less threat existed now.

The Barbary Coast a bit farther along the shoreline was packed with refugees from Australia and every other piss pot in the world. It was barely safe to ride through the streets in daylight. After dark, getting shanghaied was as good as a man could expect. And there were far worse fates than involuntary servitude aboard a China clipper awaiting the unwary from the gangs that roved the district.

They were all to be found in the streets Slocum and Valenzuela rode through at a quick trot.

More than one curious bully boy eyed them as they rode, but Slocum gave no opportunity for anything more than curious, appraising stares.

He reached the ferry just as it was loading. The large craft rocked on the choppy waves coming in off the Pacific Ocean, but this didn't hinder the crew loading on wagons, horses, and other freight to be taken across to the far northern shore.

"Wha—"

Slocum grabbed Valenzuela by the collar and dumped him on the ground. A quick punch put him out again. Livid bruises formed above the man's ear and now on his jaw. With a heave, Slocum got him to his feet and wrapped an arm around him to half drag the man aboard. They got curious looks since the wound in Valenzuela's shoulder continued to ooze blood. The red blossom had spread across his shirt front and made it appear he had been blasted with a shotgun.

"My friend got a little drunk, and there was a fight."

"Fight?" asked the sturdy sailor. "Where'd he git that wound?"

"Blue Parrot," Slocum said, naming an infamous saloon on the Embarcadero. "He damned near got himself shanghaied."

"Gonna bleed to death. If he does on the trip, just toss him over the side. Sharks're 'specially hungry today."

Slocum hunted for fare and didn't have enough. He fumbled in Valenzuela's pocket and pulled out a thick wad of greenbacks. Counting them would give close to eight hundred dollars, he guessed. He paid the sailor, made sure their horses were secured for the rough trip across, and then dropped Valenzuela to the deck.

He ran his fingers over the scrip he'd taken from the road agent.

"Swindling your own sister finally paid off—for me," Slocum said. He nudged Valenzuela with the toe of his boot to elicit some response. A moan told him the man was still alive. Slocum settled down for the trip across to Sausalito.

When the ferry docked with a loud thud against the pier, Slocum heaved Valenzuela to his feet. The man stirred and tried to fight, arms flailing about weakly. Slocum pinned his arms to his side and dragged him off and waited for their horses to be led from the ferry. The sailor gave Slocum an odd look, then returned to work on unloading freight when the ferry captain shouted for him to stop malingering.

Slocum heaved Valenzuela belly down over his saddle, then mounted and led the horse north. By the time it got dark, he had reached the junction for the road leading to the southeast and San Quentin. He felt anxious about what had to be done at dawn tomorrow. Atencio was destined to swing then, and Slocum wanted to be as close as he could to the prison to be there on time. More than this, he had to find Murrieta and see if everything he had asked for had been fetched and was ready.

If anything went wrong, there'd be a new grave in the cemetery outside the prison walls—or maybe several. Slocum didn't want to fill one of those new unmarked graves.

He rode a half mile down the road toward San Quentin, then left the road when he heard sounds ahead. He melted into the landscape just as a pair of guards from the prison trotted away, arguing about something he couldn't make out. As they vanished in the dark, he caught one snippet.

"Wilkinson said he saw somebody 'bout here."

Slocum felt a mite better. The guards riding patrol meant Sergeant Wilkinson hadn't caught anyone, so Murrieta must be around somewhere. No one else had reason to sneak around the area. If anyone came to see Atencio hanged, they would arrive in the morning on the first ferry. Although he should have asked and hadn't, Slocum reckoned that ferry would arrive a bit after dawn. He doubted the ferrymen worked in the dark because of the strong currents flowing into San Francisco Bay from the Pacific. Any mishap in the dark and rescuers would never find crew or ferry. If there would even be a rescue party sent out under any circumstances other than salvage.

He rode through the woods, stopping often to listen for either guards or Murrieta. As luck would have it, he found Murrieta in a cold camp some distance ahead.

He saw the man's dark figure rise and go for the rifle leaning against a fallen log.

"It's me," Slocum called. "I've got him." As if to acknowledge this, José Valenzuela let out a moan and began to struggle, trying to slide off the horse.

Slocum rode closer to Murrieta, then reached over, grabbed Valenzuela by the belt, and yanked. The man fell heavily and struggled to sit up.

Murrieta stepped up and swung the butt of the rifle. The impact of wooden stock against bony chin sounded like a gunshot.

"Quiet," Slocum cautioned. "Wilkinson has his men out patrolling the main road."

"I know. I have my own lookout to warn me."

"Who?" Slocum went for his six-shooter, then stopped when they were joined by another darkness-clad figure he recognized instantly. "You shouldn't have come. This is too dangerous."

"I had to," Maria said. "Procipio needed help with everything from the store."

"You got it all? No trouble?"

"John, you know me well by now. There was no problem."

Slocum had questions but found his mouth otherwise occupied with Maria's lips pressing hard. They kissed. He was aware of Murrieta watching and felt uneasy at this, but Maria did not.

"I can watch our prisoner," Murrieta said, some disdain in his voice.

Maria took Slocum by the hand and insistently pulled him out into the dark woods for privacy. His last sight of camp was Murrieta securely tying Valenzuela, and then he was otherwise delightfully occupied for the rest of the night.

Valenzuela struggled, but Murrieta had bound him well, adding a gag to be sure he wouldn't draw attention to himself until the time was right.

Slocum and Maria watched Murrieta ride away, circling the imposing prison walls with a pack animal loaded with everything from the general store.

"When do we act?" she asked.

Slocum put his finger to her lips as he heard the clatter of hooves along the road leading to the prison's front gate. They watched from a secluded spot a hundred yards away as Sheriff Bernard rode to the gate, which immediately opened.

"He came," Maria said. "He wants to see Atencio die!"

Slocum wasn't sure that was the sheriff's motive, but he said nothing. Wilkinson sent out a small platoon of guards to escort the sheriff inside. Two of the guards remained outside, both armed with rifles.

"After what happened before," Slocum said softly, although it was unlikely the guards could overhear at such a distance, "the warden's not taking any chances."

Valenzuela struggled and tried to cry out, but the gag in his mouth prevented more than a muffled sound.

"They will accept you dead as well as alive," Maria said with venom. This did nothing to still Valenzuela's struggles.

"Leave him be. The execution is scheduled for fifteen minutes," Slocum said.

"Then do it now, John. Take no chances!"

"Too soon and Atencio won't be brought out from the cell block."

"Wait too long and he will die!"

Slocum understood her anxiety, but timing was vital.

"You mount up and hightail it away," he told her. "There's no reason for you to be here now. Murrieta ought to be in position." Slocum checked his pocket watch again. Keyed up, he felt the same thrill he always had before going into battle during the war. His troops, such as they were, had been deployed . . .

"I hear chants from inside," Maria said.

"I'll be damned if the warden hasn't brought out the prisoners to watch the execution. That's the only reason for so much noise."

Slocum led Valenzuela's horse out of the thicket and fastened the reins around the saddle horn.

To Maria, he said, "I told you to get out of here. The time's right to get this started."

She gave him a quick kiss, saying, "For luck!" Then she mounted and rode away from San Quentin. Slocum counted to ten, then slapped Valenzuela's horse on the rump, sending it rocketing toward the two guards posted outside the gate.

Valenzuela did his part, wobbling in the saddle with his hands bound behind his back. Instinct kept him in the saddle when his best chance would have been to fall to the ground, then run like hell. If he had done that, Slocum would have been forced to shoot the man. But Valenzuela found himself at the gate, guards lifting their rifles to fire when Sergeant Wilkinson bellowed for them not to shoot.

"Capture him. That's one of the escapees!"

Slocum grinned. So far everything worked well with Wilkinson recognizing Valenzuela. His smile faded when Wilkinson dragged José from the saddle, plucking the gag from his mouth.

Valenzuela screamed loud enough to be heard all the way back in San Francisco, "Slocum! He's out there. In the woods!"

By now, Sheriff Bernard had come out to see what the

fuss was about. He and Wilkinson exchanged quick words, probably arguing over what Valenzuela meant. They knew him as Jarvis, but Valenzuela's insistence was enough to goad the lawmen into action.

Slocum used the time they spent discussing what was happening to mount. With his horse straining under him, Slocum bolted across the open area, where he found himself an immediate target. Both armed guards opened fire on him, Valenzuela screeching the entire time for Slocum's death as they fired.

Slocum bent low and raced after Murrieta as Wilkinson mustered his guards. Bernard found his horse first and rode to cut Slocum off, but there was little chance that would happen. More guards rushed from inside the prison. Slocum heard the warden's strident voice ordering the guards back inside to control the prisoners.

He had been right about the noise blossoming from inside the prison. The warden had assembled the prisoners to watch. There might be hundreds of them in the yard surrounding the gallows.

Slocum rode harder, striving to stay ahead of the sheriff. His horse began to tire just as he saw Murrieta waving to him. Murrieta had unloaded the packhorse and had piled the two cases of dynamite against the stone wall.

"I have it ready," Murrieta called.

Slocum glanced up. His memory was good. This stretch wasn't easily seen from either of the guard towers at either end of the wall. He hit the ground running, knowing Bernard wasn't far behind.

"You did good," he said, seeing that Murrieta had burrowed down some into the dirt to half bury the crates of dynamite. The explosion had to go inward if they were to breach the wall. Slocum whipped out his tin of lucifers, scratched one against his belt buckle, and applied the flaring tip to the fuse.

"Only six inches," Murrieta said, "as you told me."

Black miners' fuse burned at one foot per minute. Thirty seconds ought to be enough to get them safely away.

Only Sheriff Bernard had chosen this instant to gallop up, six-gun out.

"Grab some sky, you two. Now or I'll shoot!"

Slocum saw the fuse sputtering toward the blasting cap and knew they had another fifteen seconds.

"Run," he said, shoving Murrieta along the wall. "Stay with the horses!"

He dodged away from the wall to draw Bernard's fire. The sheriff didn't open up but rode closer. Slocum played for time—and won.

The dynamite erupted with a throaty roar that shook the ground and made the world stand still for an instant. Then rock, dirt, and debris exploded outward, showering Slocum where he lay facedown, arms over his head. Shaken, he rolled over and saw that the blast had knocked Bernard from his horse. Where the horse had gone, he couldn't tell. Slocum was partially deaf, and his eyes watered from the still-billowing dust cloud.

He got to his feet and ran to the six-foot hole they'd blown in the wall.

He was almost crushed by the prisoners fighting to escape through the hole. Slocum grabbed the men and heaved them from his path, forcing himself into the prison. He felt like a fish swimming up a fast-running stream.

Some prisoners fought with guards, but most tried to get free through the hole that had miraculously opened for them.

Slocum made his way toward the gallows but saw Warden Harriman on the platform, hand on the lever that would spring the trap under his black-hooded prisoner. Atencio was only seconds away from being hanged.

18

Jostled about as he was, Slocum knew he would have a hard time getting a good shot at the warden. Worse, if he missed and only winged the man, he might jerk away and throw the lever, guaranteeing Atencio's death.

The prisoners all around him were attacking and being attacked by the guards. He pushed forward, desperately hoping that he could reach the gallows before Harriman carried out the death sentence.

Then Slocum heard a high-pitched voice that cut through the din like a knife.

"Stop! Do not kill him!"

Maria rode through the crowd straight for the gallows. It took Slocum a few seconds to realize someone had opened the main gate, giving her the chance to ride in. But she was oblivious to the fight raging all around her and did not realize how enticing it was to an escaping prisoner to ride out on a horse—her horse.

Slocum was torn between helping Maria and saving Atencio from the warden's easy movement of the lever controlling the trapdoor. He made his decision and fought his way toward the woman.

He clubbed one prisoner trying to pull her from the saddle and kicked another out of her way. The prisoners realized they couldn't remain inside the walls long or they would be trapped again when Sergeant Wilkinson got his men under control. Right now, the guards fought as individuals and not as a well-disciplined unit. When that changed, they would begin rounding up the prisoners in a methodical fashion, starting with those still inside the walls. Tracking those who had successfully breached the walls would take more time.

Wilkinson would want to hang on to what prisoners he could. The guard sergeant might be many things, but Slocum doubted he was incompetent. San Quentin had been run too efficiently for too long to believe Wilkinson wasn't capable of clever planning or even outright brutality when it was called for.

"Go to him," Maria cried when she saw Slocum trying to clear the way for her. "You can stop the warden. I cannot!"

"Yes, you can," Slocum said. "You caught the warden by surprise. Play on that. Beg him to release Atencio. I'll be right behind you."

Slocum followed the woman through the thinning fight. Guards were beginning to gain the upper hand as prisoners realized it was better for them to run than fight.

"Please, I beg you. He is innocent!" Maria sat astride her horse and looked up the few feet to the warden, who simply stared at her as if he had never seen a woman before in his life.

"How'd you get in here?" Harriman finally asked.

The hesitation on his part and her slowness to answer him gave Slocum time to get around to the steps leading to the execution platform. While Maria distracted the warden,

Slocum took the steps two at a time to reach the top of the gallows. Only then did the warden realize what was happening.

He tried to throw the lever, but Slocum was already swinging. His meaty fist struck the warden on the cheek and sent him reeling. Slocum quickly followed up with a haymaker that knocked Harriman off the platform. He fell heavily to the ground fifteen feet below. He landed flat on his back. The loud whoosh of breath gusting from his lungs carried over the din of battle throughout the prison yard.

Slocum wasted no time getting the hood off Atencio's head and then lifting the noose from his neck.

"*Gracias* . . ." the man started. Slocum didn't let him get any farther. He slammed his palm against the lever.

Both of them hurtled downward and landed heavily under the gallows floor. Slocum caught the man because his ankles were bound together.

"Let me get you free."

"Why did you—"

"Wilkinson's alerted the guards in the towers. They're going to open fire at any instant."

The words had barely escaped his lips when the sharp report from a half-dozen rifles filled the prison yard.

Slocum slit the ropes and helped Atencio take a step or two until he got circulation back into his legs.

"What do we do?"

Slocum hadn't thought this far ahead. In none of his schemes had he considered a riot and mass escape.

"Get behind Maria and ride the hell out of here," Slocum said.

"Maria? She is here?" Atencio's eyes went wide and a broad, toothy grin split his face. "I knew she would come for me!"

Slocum grabbed him by the arm and pulled him from

under the gallows. As they rounded the base, the warden struggled to his feet, gasping out commands that brought nearby guards running to him.

"Damn," Slocum muttered under his breath. He kept moving and hunted for Maria, but the woman had disappeared.

"Where is she? Where?"

"She must have hightailed it out of the prison. She pulled your fat from the fire by distracting the warden." Slocum saw that Sergeant Wilkinson was closing the main gate, cutting off escape that way. He hoped Maria had ridden away because being trapped on this side of the wall would be a terrible fate for her.

"We've got to get out the hole I blasted. Murrieta is on the other side."

"Procipio? He came to save me also?" This pleased Atencio even more.

Slocum wanted to give him time to thank his friends, but they had to first get out of the prison yard. Barely had he gone a dozen paces when he realized the hole he had blown in the wall was closed off by four armed guards. He started to draw and shoot his way out, then realized that would draw attention to him. The tower guards had stopped firing but were still where they could ventilate him if necessary.

"We can't go that way," he said. Grabbing Atencio and shoving him in the direction of the cell block was the only thing he could do. To remain out in the open meant their capture.

Slocum vowed not to let them take him alive. He had spent almost a week in solitary and wasn't going to do that again. Sergeant Wilkinson still thought he was Jasper Jarvis and an escapee. No amount of argument would change that. Worse, the only lawyer he knew of had stolen money intended to bribe a judge to free Atencio. He was entirely on his own.

"They will not let us stay inside," Atencio said with such assurance that Slocum almost believed him. Almost.

Then he saw how Wilkinson roamed the ranks of the guards and swept through the yard, collecting any convict who had been unlucky enough to remain inside. The truncheons swung and heads were split open. The bloody tide moved inexorably.

"Into the cell block," Slocum said. "It's our only way to get out."

"How? There is nothing but . . . cells."

Slocum wasn't sure, but since this was his only route left, he had to take it. He and Atencio slipped through the open door and into the holding area. Slocum remembered it only too well. From here he had been herded to the room where he was scrubbed down and given the prison uniform.

"Uniforms," Slocum said.

"*Sí*, yes, I have one on." Atencio grabbed the heavy canvas of the striped shirt and held it out. "They would bury me in this, the pigs."

"Guards' uniforms. Where can we find some?" He had gotten into the prison before by pretending to be a guard. It was a long shot but all he had if they were to get out.

"I do not know. There, perhaps. The guards have bunks there."

Slocum didn't wait to see if Atencio followed him. He ran for the door and kicked it open, ready to gun down any guard who might be inside. The room was empty. Bunks lined two walls and at the far end were hooks, some with guard uniforms dangling from them. Hardly breaking stride after kicking the door, Slocum reached the clothing and quickly sized up the blue wool coats and trousers with the dull brass buttons.

"Here," he said, tossing a set over his shoulder to Atencio. "Put it on over your prison uniform. No time to strip." As he spoke, he found a uniform for himself that was several sizes too big. This worked to his advantage. He tightened a belt around his middle so that the pant legs dropped far enough down to cover the tops of his boots. The coat went on and hid his cross-draw holster with the ebony-handled six-shooter in it. He sent his hat sailing under a bunk and tried on three caps before he found one that didn't perch on the top of his head like a bird hatching an egg.

"You look silly," Atencio said.

"So do you. Let's hope we don't die laughing."

Slocum returned to the door and peered out into the holding pen. Four guards had come in, all armed with their sticks but no guns. He considered taking them, but the sound would bring other guards running.

He took the bull by the horns.

"Where's the sarge?" Slocum bellowed. "I gotta talk to him."

"How's that?"

"Wilkinson, you dimwit. Where's Sergeant Wilkinson? I heard there's a tunnel being dug outta here."

"Who the hell cares about a tunnel? We have a riot and jailbreak on our hands," one guard said.

"He'll want to know. Them that's not got away already can escape in the tunnel."

The guards exchanged puzzled looks.

"Get on down to solitary and see if I'm not right. At the far end, out through a cell wall. Looks like they're making a beeline north."

The four grumbled but vanished down stairs Slocum hadn't even noticed before. He went to the top of the stairs and saw a door open. From below he heard the cries of prisoners in solitary, begging for food or warmth or to be let out or just to die.

Slocum grabbed the door and pulled it shut but could not lock it without a key.

"They'll be back up here in a minute or two. We have to be long gone."

"They are bringing in the prisoners they recaptured. Where can we hide?"

"With the guards, that's where. Keep your face down and hope none of the prisoners rats you out."

Just then the doors opened and the prisoners crowded through, herded by the guards with their truncheons whacking asses and heads and any other slow-moving portion of their jailbirds' anatomy. Slocum shouted and shoved the prisoners along, stooping to pick up a truncheon he saw lying on the floor.

Atencio lowered his face, muttered under his breath, and tried to duplicate everything Slocum did. Their act was unconvincing, but the confusion of returning so many prisoners to their cells kept them from being noticed.

As they passed a corridor leading away into the heart of the cell block, Slocum shoved Atencio from the crowd.

"We cannot do this," Atencio whispered as he walked shoulder to shoulder with Slocum. "This is the office of the warden. We will be found quickly!"

Slocum didn't bother answering. He needed some advantage and thought this might pay off for them. The door with the name plate WARDEN HARRIMAN was locked, but he forced it with his knife. He didn't care if the warden noticed the sprung lock or not.

"This is such a fine place, no?" Atencio went to a table and pulled the cork from a bottle of wine. He upended it and drained what remained in the bottle in a single gulp. "I have lived so long without wine. This is good. Where is there more?"

"Don't get drunk," Slocum said as he dropped into the chair behind the warden's desk. The drawers were locked but yielded to his thick-bladed knife. He rummaged through hunting for something—anything—useful and found nothing but papers.

"Why not? Never will we escape this accursed place."

Atencio found a second bottle, this one full, and worried the cork out of the neck with his teeth. Before he could get down to the serious work of draining the bottle, sounds in the corridor alerted them.

Slocum pointed to a spot behind the door. Atencio took up his post there, the empty wine bottle gripped hard to use as a club.

"I don't care what it costs. I want them all back in their cells by midnight!" Warden Harriman stormed into his office, then stopped, hands still on the doorknob as it slowly penetrated something was wrong.

Slocum leaned back in the warden's chair and said nothing.

"Get out of my chair," Harriman snapped. "You can't— wait! The lock's broken. You're not going to steal anything from *my* office!"

Slocum nodded and Atencio kicked the door shut, sending Harriman staggering. Then Atencio pressed hard to hold the office door shut against anyone trying to follow the warden.

Slocum drew his six-gun and aimed it at the warden as the man went for a small hideout pistol.

"You don't want to die like this. Give him your gun," Slocum ordered.

Atencio grabbed the gun from Harriman and stepped away. He cocked the pistol, obviously intending to put a bullet in the head of the man who'd almost executed him.

"Stop," Slocum said sharply. "We need him to get out of here."

"I want him dead."

"No. No killing."

"What are you, a lily-livered coward who can't shoot an unarmed man?" Harriman laughed hard, pointing at Atencio.

"He's trying to goad you," Slocum said.

"We will use him to get away," Atencio finally said, swallowing his anger with obvious effort. "How do we do this?"

"Think any of his guards want him dead?" Slocum saw the flash of fear cross Harriman's face. "Might be you can stay alive awhile longer if you keep them at bay." Slocum rounded the desk and jammed his six-shooter into the warden's ribs. He pulled his coat out enough to hide the weapon.

Using the barrel, he steered the warden out of the office. Atencio stared hard, then yielded his position, falling in on the other side of the warden as they went into the corridor where a half-dozen guards milled about.

"What are you layabouts doing here?" The warden bellowed again to get the men moving.

Slocum moved fast, knowing he had little time before Harriman figured out some way of alerting his guards. If the warden ever considered his chances less with Slocum and Atencio than he did with his own men, he would call out for help.

"I won't let him kill you," Slocum said softly, steering Harriman out into the prison yard. "I won't unless you try to get away."

"What are you going to do with me?"

"That depends," Slocum told the warden, "on how fast you can get all three of us horses to ride through that big gate."

Atencio kept his face down so the guards wouldn't notice, but the uniform proved a good disguise. The men cleaning up the yard, hunting for hiding prisoners, and working to get back a semblance of discipline saw only the blue coat and the garrison cap, not the face.

"Where are you going, Warden?"

Slocum tensed. He recognized Sergeant Wilkinson's raspy voice.

"Tell him you're going to supervise the hunt outside the walls."

Harriman spoke in a monotone voice that caused Wilkinson to come over.

"Something wrong, Warden?"

Slocum considered just shooting the guard sergeant, then knew that would only get him and Atencio killed on the spot. As good as it would feel to cut down Wilkinson, the feeling would be short-lived once the tower guards opened fire on them.

"Nothing, nothing's wrong. Get me those horses. Th-These men and I will find the escapees since you are unable to do so."

"We just started, and those yahoos can't get far," Wilkinson said.

"No back talk, Sergeant!"

Wilkinson went off, grumbling. Slocum relaxed a little and told the warden, "You saved both your lives."

"Go to hell. I'll see both of you on the gallows with your damned necks broken! Mark my words!"

A guard brought up three saddled horses. Slocum found himself jockeying around so the warden would mount under the cover of the six-shooter but had to mount himself. In those seconds there wouldn't be anything to keep Harriman in line.

"Kill him if he tries to warn the guards," Slocum whispered to Atencio loud enough for the warden to overhear. "Use that derringer you took from him. It's not much of a gun, but you've got two shots."

Harriman started to kick his heels into his horse's flanks, but the threat slowed him long enough for Slocum to mount and cover him again.

"Out. Now. Take it slow. Order the gates open."

Slocum and Atencio rode knee to knee with Harriman to keep him in line. The hair on the back of Slocum's neck rose as they approached the gate. So close to getting out of San Quentin. So close.

The gate swung open, and they started forward.

"Hold on! Stop them!" came Wilkinson's order.

They'd been discovered.

19

"Run for it!" Atencio galloped away, leaving Slocum and Harriman in the dust. Slocum wanted to duplicate that escape effort but held back. Outrunning a posse of guards from the prison wasn't possible.

"Wilkinson!" Harriman half turned in the saddle. He stopped when he saw the gunmetal blue of Slocum's Colt. The muzzle pointed directly at his belly.

"Keep your wits about you, and I won't spill your guts all over the ground."

"I'll have you back, Jarvis. I swear it!"

"Say anything wrong and you'll never live to see me anywhere but in hell."

Slocum's cold tone caused the warden to suck in his breath. He turned the rest of the way in the saddle to face his sergeant.

"Warden, we got word."

"What are you going on about?" Harriman glanced at Slocum and the pistol, then back at his guard.

"Some of the men heard 'bout a tunnel from the solitary cells out under the wall. That might be where some of the prisoners went."

"Have you seen the tunnel with your own eyes?" Harriman sounded genuinely pained at the notion of his prisoners being clever enough to tunnel out under his nose.

"Can't find it. Do I have your permission to loosen some of the stones in the walls to hunt for it?"

Harriman looked hard at Slocum, then nodded brusquely.

"We need to tighten security, sir," Wilkinson said. "There's no telling how many of them thievin', murderin' bastards might have gone out that way."

"Plug the hole, Sergeant. Whatever it takes."

"Yes, sir." Wilkinson started to go back into the prison yard, then stopped.

Slocum's finger tightened on the trigger. First he would kill Harriman, then Wilkinson. From there it would be a race to get away, but at least two of them from San Quentin would pay for all they'd done to him during the eternity he'd spent in solitary confinement.

"Is there something wrong, Warden?" Wilkinson took a step back. Slocum didn't have to know the sergeant was eyeing him hard. "Come on back, and I'll show you where the tunnel's supposed to be."

"Get on with your job, Wilkinson. I'll see to rounding up the escapees out here."

"Sir, I—"

"Do as I order, Sergeant Wilkinson!" The warden's voice rose and almost cracked with strain. "I cannot have my prisoners roaming the countryside one instant longer than needful."

"Yes, sir, but—"

Harriman pointedly turned his back. Slocum gestured with the gun, and the warden rode ahead at a trot. Never looking back, Slocum caught up.

"Don't bother looking to Wilkinson for help," Slocum said. "You did good. You kept him alive. Yourself, too."

"I'll personally throw the trapdoor on the gallows for you, Jarvis. I swear it!"

Slocum let the warden rant on until they came to the junction in the road. The left fork went back to the San Francisco ferry. Since he had no idea about the schedule, Slocum couldn't afford to wait long there. Closer down another peninsula was the Tiburon ferry. Its schedule was a mystery, too. He had no choice but to ride north.

The lure of Oregon called powerfully. Anything to be away from California and San Quentin. But he had to make sure he had plenty of time.

"Off your horse," Slocum ordered. "Now take off your shoes." He had Harriman tie the laces together and drape them over the now riderless horse. By the time the warden hobbled back to the prison, Slocum hoped to be long gone.

"You're not going to kill me?"

"I've done my share of killing," Slocum said, "during the war and after. Never killed a man who wasn't trying to kill me."

"I said I'd see you hanged."

Slocum laughed. "You trying to get me to shoot you? Start running. That way, toward the San Francisco ferry."

Harriman hesitated, then saw how Slocum sighted along his barrel. He took off at a dead run. Slocum watched him for a minute until he disappeared around a bend in the road, then swung his horse around and galloped north. He held the reins to the other horse to keep it close by. When the horse he rode tired, Slocum switched horses. He shucked off the guard uniform and kept riding hard until he saw how the shoreline bent around and back southward.

He knew better than to poke his nose back San Francisco way, but he had unfinished business. Just the thought of that business made him run eager fingers over the worn handle of his six-shooter.

* * *

"Not sure when the ferry'll be across, mister," the port agent said.

Slocum looked across the Bay but couldn't see San Francisco through a thin veil of fog. He considered giving up on his quest for vengeance and clearing out. Oakland wasn't his kind of town, and San Francisco might be too hot to bear, no matter how much he wanted to put a bullet in José Valenzuela for all he had done.

He worried that his sudden concern for revenge might be tied up with wanting to see Maria again, too. Atencio had lit out like his ass was on fire. Slocum hoped he had gotten back to Murrieta's small village, where they could hide him until the man could escape south to Mexico. Going back to find out would put him in jeopardy, though, from both Harriman and Sheriff Bernard.

"You wanna ticket or no?" the agent asked.

Slocum started to say no when he heard a whistle from out on the Bay.

"You're in luck. That there's the *Berkeley Delight* comin' over from Frisco. Won't be but a half hour 'fore she heads back."

Slocum silently paid for the ticket, damning himself as a fool the entire time. He tucked the cardboard stub in his coat pocket and went to find a place to sit until the ferry unloaded and he could board. But he sat a mite straighter when he saw the first passenger off the ferry.

José Valenzuela kept his face down and almost ran, though clearly still in pain, as he tugged on the reins to keep his skittish horse moving. When he was well off the ramp leading to the ferry's deck, he vaulted into the saddle and galloped away, scattering pedestrians and gaining their angry curses and gestures.

It took Slocum less time than that to step up into the saddle. He left his spare horse tethered as he raced after Valenzuela, getting the same gestures and curses the fleeing outlaw had. Slocum concentrated on keeping Valenzuela in

sight as he wound through the Oakland streets and finally
stopped at a hotel that had seen better days.

Slocum had to take a quick turn when Valenzuela
stepped into the street, hand on six-gun thrust into his belt,
and looked to see if anyone had followed. The wicked
might flee when no man pursued, but in this case it was
John Slocum pursuing the wicked. Satisfied he had evaded
anyone on his trail, Valenzuela swaggered into the hotel.

Hastily dismounting and going to the boardwalk outside the open hotel door, Slocum caught the last part of
Valenzuela's argument with the clerk.

"She is my sister. Not that it matters to you." Valenzuela
drew his six-shooter and laid it on the counter. "What room
is she in?"

"Mister, we got brothers and sisters stayin' here all the
time. I'm tellin' you she ain't in, and I ain't lettin' you in
her room 'less she says it's all right."

"I will—" Valenzuela cut off his angry tirade when
Conchita came from the hotel dining room, drawn by his
loud voice. *"¡Hermana!"*

They embraced, speaking in low, rapid Spanish that
Slocum could not follow. He peered around the door frame
as they continued to talk. Finally Conchita pointed toward
the dining room and José followed.

Slocum waited a few minutes, then entered, going
straight to the clerk.

"I'm looking for friends of mine. The Valenzuelas," he
said.

The clerk gave him a sour look, then spit into a cuspi-
dor behind the counter.

"They're eatin'."

"All three of them?"

"Yeah, the lady and the old coot. And the lady's
brother," the clerk said, as if he didn't believe José.

Slocum had heard all he needed to know. The entire

Valenzuela clan was holed up here. But where was the loot they had taken from the Miramar bank and the stage?

"There they are, just now comin' from the restaurant. Hey!" The clerk started to hail the outlaws, but Slocum was quicker.

He grabbed the clerk's wrist and slammed the hand down hard on the counter.

"I want to surprise them. Don't let on I know them."

"Son of a bitch," the clerk muttered. "They ain't been nuthin' but trouble, and she was so purty, too. Oughta know by now, the purty ones're always trouble."

"Are they looking this way?" Slocum asked.

"Naw, they went upstairs. Leastways, the brother and sister did. They left the old coot at the foot of the stairs."

"Thanks," Slocum said, keeping his back to the elder Valenzuela as he went outside, then ran down the street to where he'd left his horse. Barely breaking stride, he vaulted into the saddle. The horse shied, but Slocum clung on. He sat upright and saw the Valenzuelas coming from the hotel.

A smile crept across Slocum's face. José lugged a heavy box and Conchita wrestled with a carpetbag about big enough for all the greenbacks stolen from the stage. If José carried a box laden with gold, Slocum saw his reward. He half drew his six-gun, then slid it back into the holster. A better plan than simply robbing the Valenzuelas came to him.

They worked to get their burden settled on the back of a horse, then the trio mounted and rode into the hills, the packhorse dutifully plodding along behind. Slocum kept his distance because he knew José would be as nervy as a rotten tooth, jumping at every sound or sight that might mean they were being trailed.

Although much of the way lay along a road, it wended higher into the hills and provided Slocum enough cover to follow close enough to make sure they didn't suddenly vanish on him. From their determination, he knew what they intended. They were going to hide the stolen loot.

Twilight hid details along the trail as they continued higher into the hills, then down into a valley when Conchita pointed out the trail to her brother. She had scouted this area and now directed José to where they'd hide their ill-gotten gold.

When the trio cut away from the trail, working higher into the rocky hills, Slocum left the trail, too, and advanced on foot after hiding his horse in a thicket. By the time he reached the spot where the Valenzuelas stood in a half circle around a pile of rocks, they had finished their work.

"We can retrieve it when we please," Conchita said.

José agreed. Slocum wondered if the man intended to double-cross his sister again. He had cheated her out of eight hundred dollars when Slocum had kidnapped their pa. Or was José limited to such petty thievery? Conchita would be implacable hunting him down if he stole from her. José had to know that. If he intended to keep the loot for himself, he needed a scapegoat.

Their pa was the only one likely to fit that bill, and Slocum doubted Conchita would believe for an instant the murderous, nearsighted *viejo* would do such a thing—or could do it.

They tossed a few more rocks on the pile, then mounted and rode off, laughing and joking.

Slocum waited fifteen minutes to be sure they had truly gone before beginning to root around under the rocks. They had hidden their treasure well, but he found it.

Pulling out the carpetbag, he held it up in the last of daylight and saw stacks of greenbacks inside. The crate José had carried proved more difficult to open, but when he did, it seemed that the gold coins inside shone with a light of their own.

Slocum was finally well paid for all he had been through.

But he couldn't carry it all away, not when it had taken a pack animal to get it up here. He began the tedious process of finding a new hiding place as far as possible from where the Valenzuelas had buried their gold. It was well past midnight before he had carefully erased his tracks and made sure his new cache was well concealed.

Then he rode back to Oakland. He still had a ferry ticket.

20

Slocum rode off the ferry a little after dawn. The time he spent waiting to cross San Francisco Bay he had gloated over stealing the loot from the Valenzuelas. That left a warm spot in his belly and gave him even more reason to dare crossing paths with the law on the San Francisco side of the Bay. Maria might take some persuading, but Slocum wanted her to come with him. Maybe not to Oregon but away from California now that Atencio had been freed. There was no reason for her to stay in Murrieta's village grubbing beans out of the ground when she could live in style.

He had to wonder if she would ever ask about the source of Slocum's newfound wealth. What would he tell her if she did ask? She was an honest woman and might not cotton much to spending money that had been stolen from the bank. The banker had stolen much of what had been in his vault from the *peones* in the village. Slocum considered using some of the gold to pay off those mort-gages. Maria would like that.

"Git yerse'ves off. Ferry goes back to Oakland in twenty

minutes," bellowed a dockhand. Slocum didn't have to be told twice. He had an hour's ride ahead of him getting south of the city to see Maria again.

As he rode from the Embarcadero, he got an uneasy feeling and looked around. He immediately pulled down his hat to hide his face. Two uniformed guards lounged about not far from the docks. He recognized one from San Quentin, even if he hadn't spotted their outfits. Warden Harriman had yet to catch all the escaped prisoners and kept watch to be sure none left town on the ferry.

All that saved Slocum from being noticed was that he came from Oakland. Getting back on the ferry might be chancy if the prison guards continued their vigilance. Slocum turned the corner and trotted toward Portsmouth Square, the guards still watching travelers getting onto the ferry. He didn't dare come back this way. Better to ride far south and follow the Bay until the shoreline turned north again so he could retrieve the money he had left hidden in the hills above Oakland.

A new warmth suffused him. He had robbed the Valenzuelas and wanted to be there when they discovered they were again poor. Slocum knew that he was unlikely to witness it, but the image of them blaming each other made him smile. The smile turned to a toothy grin when a new idea came to him how to really ruin their day.

He rode around until he found a telegraph office. Inside, he dictated the telegram to Harriman where he could find one of his escaped prisoners. That would get José Valenzuela clapped back in the penitentiary where he belonged. Helping Harriman was a thorn in his side, but the irritation passed quickly knowing Conchita would have to visit her brother behind bars once more.

She wasn't likely to find another dupe to break him out either. Harriman's recent setbacks as warden would force him to lock down San Quentin so hard that a flea couldn't get out.

"Confusion to my enemies," Slocum said, shoving the flimsy yellow sheet to the telegrapher. The man looked up, cocked his head to one side, and stared at him.

"You want that added to the 'gram?"

"Send it, as is. If the warden or, more likely, a guard sergeant named Wilkinson comes by asking about who sent the message, you might get yourself a reward if you say that you overheard this in a bar." Slocum tapped the message with his forefinger.

"And if I mention you to this sergeant?"

Slocum shifted his weight slightly so his left hip was thrust out. The telegrapher took in the well-used handle of the Colt Navy and Slocum's obvious readiness to use that formidable weapon.

"You figger somebody's gonna come by to inquire?"

Slocum only nodded.

"That'll be a dollar-ten to send the 'gram."

Slocum slid across a twenty-dollar greenback.

"Keep the change," he said.

The telegrapher took a deep breath and made the bill vanish as fast as a frog's tongue snares a fly in midair.

"You want me to wait 'fore I send this?"

"Now," Slocum said. "I want you send it right now."

The telegrapher dropped the sheet on his desk, sent a preliminary few clicks, then settled down to converting the letters into code. Slocum left while he was still in the middle of sending.

He mounted and rode off, feeling even better about himself. Letting Harriman know where to find José Valenzuela had so many advantages.

Slocum's caution saved him from riding straight into the village and into Sheriff Bernard's arms. The lawman had a small posse spread about the village, going house to house. Slocum tethered his horse some distance away, then hiked to the top of a hill where he could flop on his belly and watch the progress as Bernard hunted for outlaws. Or had he joined the search for the San Quentin escapees?

It might be that Bernard just hunted for local law-breakers and to hell with the escapees.

After an hour, Bernard shooed his men from the village and trotted back to the main road. Where he went with his search then was something Slocum had to worry over. The sheriff still wanted him for a variety of crimes. A new smile curled his lips. He hadn't robbed Galworthy's bank, but he had ended up with the loot. That made him as guilty as the Valenzuelas, he reckoned, but Slocum wasn't going to lose any sleep over legal carping.

He hiked to the village and walked in, leaving his horse hidden in the hills. Slocum looked around for any sign that Bernard had followed Harriman's lead and had posted deputies to watch for escaped prisoners.

Procipio Murrieta came from his house, stopped, and stared when he saw Slocum. His mouth opened, then he clamped it shut.

"Took a spell for me to get back," Slocum said. "I had to wait for the sheriff to leave. He giving you any trouble?"

"He and I have come to an agreement. He cares nothing for what happens in San Quentin. Still, I chose to stay away while he searched."

"I got that feeling he wasn't inclined to do Harriman's work for him," Slocum said. "So he's not looking for me?"

"He still believes you are the one who robbed the bank." Murrieta cleared his throat, then said, "And yes, he seeks you here. You must go immediately. The sheriff is like a dog with a bone. He will never stop gnawing. That makes it dangerous for you—and the village—if you remain any longer."

"I need to talk to you about that," Slocum said. "But I want to see Maria first." He saw the play of emotion on Murrieta's face and tensed. "She wasn't hurt, was she?

Wilkinson or Harriman isn't using her to catch Atencio?"

Murrieta shook his head, then reached out and took Slocum by the arm, walking him to the town plaza, where the well provided a gathering spot.

"She is . . . not here. She has become frightened and ran away."

"What scared her?"

Slocum saw the new play of emotion and knew whatever Murrieta said would be a lie.

"I frighten her with new plans. I seek to arm my people. We must fight. We . . . we are planning to revolt against the laws that oppress us."

"Where'd she go?"

"Away. Far away. I do not know where. Perhaps south to Mexico."

Slocum looked past Murrieta's shoulder and saw Maria and Atencio across the plaza. They had their arms wrapped around each other and had eyes only for the other.

"Who is Atencio to her?"

Murrieta paused, licked his lips, and finally said, "You have been a good man and have done much for me and my people. I do not want to lie to you."

"Then don't," Slocum said coldly.

"Atencio is her husband. They have been married for almost a year."

"Happily?"

Murrieta nodded.

"She carries his child."

More words wouldn't come.

Slocum saw Maria and Atencio disappear into a small house on the far side of the plaza. A light inside extinguished, and the door closed with a loud slam. He imagined laughter—Maria's—as Atencio took her to bed. Their bed. Their marriage bed.

"Take care," Slocum said.

"Please, do not go away angry at her. She had no other way to get him free."

"They shouldn't stay here. Even if the sheriff looks the other way when Harriman or Wilkinson asks about escapees, he's likely to arrest Atencio eventually."

"That is so," Murrieta said.

Slocum shook the man's hand, turned, and went into the twilight to find his horse. Riding back to San Francisco for the ferry would be dangerous. Skirting the Bay to the south and then entering Oakland that way would take a day or two, but he wasn't in a hurry.

He had a lot to think over as he went to retrieve the gold he had hidden. Wherever he went after stashing it all in his saddlebags had to be far, far away. Far from San Quentin, from the Valenzuelas, and especially from Maria.